BOSAMBO
OF THE RIVER

BY

EDGAR WALLACE

Author of "Sanders of the River," "People of the River,"
"Four Just Men," etc.

WARD, LOCK & CO., LIMITED
LONDON AND MELBOURNE

CONTENTS.

BOSAMBO

OF THE RIVER

---◆---

CHAPTER I

ARACHI THE BORROWER

MANY years ago the Monrovian Government
sent one Bosambo, a native of the Kroo
coast and consequently a thief, to penal
servitude for the term of his natural life. Bosambo,
who had other views on the matter, was given
an axe and a saw in the penal settlement—which
was a patch of wild forest in the back country—
and told to cut down and trim certain mahogany-
trees in company with other unfortunate men
similarly circumstanced.

To assure themselves of Bosambo's obedience,
the Government of Liberia set over him a number
of compatriots, armed with weapons which had
rendered good service at Gettysburg, and had been
presented to the President of Liberia by President

Grant. They were picturesque weapons, but they were somewhat deficient in accuracy, especially when handled by the inexpert soldiers of the Monrovian coast. Bosambo, who put his axe to an ignoble use, no less than the slaying of Captain Peter Cole—who was as black as the ten of clubs, but a gentleman by the Liberian code—left the penal settlement with passionate haste. The Gettysburg relics made fairly good practice up to two hundred yards, but Bosambo was a mile away before the guards, searching the body of their dead commander for the key of the ammunition store, had secured food for their lethal weapons.

The government offered a reward of two hundred and fifty dollars for Bosambo, dead or alive. But, although the reward was claimed and paid to the half-brother of the Secretary of War, it is a fact that Bosambo was never caught.

On the contrary, he made his way to a far land, and became, by virtue of his attainments, chief of the Ochori.

Bosambo was too good a sportsman to leave his persecutors at peace. There can be little doubt that the Kroo insurrection, which cost the Liberian Government eight hundred and twenty-one pounds sixteen shillings to suppress, was due to the instigation and assistance of Bosambo. Of this insurrection, and the part that Bosambo played, it may be necessary to speak again.

The second rebellion was a more serious and expensive affair; and it was at the conclusion of this that the Liberian Government made representations to Britain. Sanders, who conducted an independent inquiry into the question of Bosambo's complicity, reported that there was no evidence whatever that Bosambo was directly or indirectly responsible. And with that the Liberian Government was forced to be content ; but they expressed their feelings by offering a reward of two thousand dollars for Bosambo alive or dead—preferably alive. They added, for the benefit of minor government officials and their neighbours, that they would, in the language of the advertisement, reject all substitutes. The news of this price went up and down the coast and very far into the interior, yet strangely enough Arachi of the Isisi did not learn of it until many years afterward.

Arachi was of the Isisi people, and a great borrower. Up and down the river all men knew him for such, so that his name passed into the legendary vocabulary of the people whilst he yet lived ; and did the wife of Yoka beg from the wife of O'taki the service of a cooking-pot, be sure that O'taki's wife would agree, but with heavy pleasantry scream after the retiring pot : " O thou shameless Arachi ! " whereupon all the village folk who heard the jest would rock with laughter.

Arachi was the son of a chief, but in a country where chieftainship was not hereditary, and where, moreover, many chiefs' sons dwelt without distinction, his parentage was of little advantage. Certainly it did not serve him as, in his heart, he thought he should be served.

He was tall and thin, and his knees were curiously knobbly. He carried his head on one side importantly, and was profoundly contemptuous of his fellows.

Once he came to Sanders.

"Lord," he said, "I am a chief's son, as you know, and I am very wise. Men who look upon me say, 'Behold, this young man is full of craft,' because of my looks. Also I am a great talker."

"There are many in this land who are great talkers, Arachi," said Sanders, unpleasantly; "yet they do not travel for two days down-stream to tell me so."

"Master," said Arachi impressively, "I came to you because I desire advancement. Many of your little chiefs are fools, and, moreover, unworthy. Now I am the son of a chief, and it is my wish to sit down in the place of my father. Also, lord, remember this, that I have dwelt among foreign people, the Angola folk, and speak their tongue."

Sanders sighed wearily.

"Seven times you have asked me, Arachi," he said, "and seven times I have told you you are no chief for me. Now I tell you this—that I am tired of seeing you, and if you come to me again I will throw you to the monkeys.* As for your Angola palaver, I tell you this—that if it happen—which may all gods forbid!—that a tribe of Angola folk sit down with me, you shall be chief."

* Colloquial: "Make you look foolish."

Unabashed, Arachi returned to his village, for he thought in his heart that Sandi was jealous of his great powers. He built a large hut at the end of the village, borrowing his friends' labour ; this he furnished with skins and the like, and laid in stores of salt and corn, all of which he had secured from neighbouring villages by judicious promises of payment.

It was like a king's hut, so glorious were the hangings of skin and the stretched bed of hide, and the people of his village said " Ko ! " believing that Arachi had dug up those hidden treasures which every chief is popularly supposed to possess in secret places to which his sons may well be privy.

Even those who had helped to supply the magnificence were impressed and comforted.

" I have lent Arachi two bags of salt," said Pidini, the chief of Kolombolo, the fishing village, " and my stomach was full of doubt, though he swore by Death that he would repay me three days after the rains. Now I see that he is indeed very rich, as he told me he was, and if my salt does not return to me I may seize his fine bed."

In another village across the River Ombili, a headman of the Isisi confided to his wife :

" Woman, you have seen the hut of Arachi, now I think you will cease your foolish talk. For you have reproached me bitterly because I lent Arachi my fine bed."

" Lord, I was wrong," said the woman meekly ; " but I feared he would not pay you the salt he promised ; now I know that I was foolish, for I saw many bags of salt in his hut."

The story of Arachi's state spread up and down the river, and when the borrower demanded the hand of Korari, the daughter of the chief of the Putani ("The Fishers of the River"), she came to him without much palaver, though she was rather young.

A straight and winsome girl well worth the thousand rods and the twenty bags of salt which the munificent Arachi promised, by Death, devils, and a variety of gods, should be delivered to her father when the moon and the river stood in certain relative positions.

Now Arachi did no manner of work whatever, save to walk through the village street at certain hours clad in a robe of monkey tails which he had borrowed from the brother of the king of the Isisi.

He neither fished nor hunted nor dug in the fields.

He talked to Korari his wife, and explained why this was so. He talked to her from sunset until the early hours of the morning, for he was a great talker, and when he was on his favourite subject—which was Arachi—he was very eloquent. He talked to her till the poor child's head rocked from side to side, and from front to back, in her desperate sleepiness.

He was a great man, beloved and trusted of Sandi. He had immense thoughts and plans— plans that would ensure him a life of ease without the distressing effects of labour. Also, Sanders would make him chief—in good time.

She should be as a queen—she would much rather have been in her bed and asleep.

Though no Christian, Arachi was a believer in miracles. He pinned his faith to the supreme miracle of living without work, and was near to seeing the fulfilment of that wonder.

But the miracle which steadfastly refused to happen was the miracle which would bring him relief at the moment when his numerous creditors were clamouring for the repayment of the many and various articles which they had placed in his care.

It is an axiom that the hour brings its man— most assuredly it brings its creditor.

There was a tumultuous and stormy day when the wrathful benefactors of Arachi gathered in full strength and took from him all that was takable, and this in the face of the village, to Korari's great shame. Arachi, on the contrary, because of his high spirit, was neither ashamed nor distressed, even though many men spoke harshly.

" O thief and rat ! " said the exasperated owner of a magnificent stool of ceremony, the base of which Arachi had contrived to burn. " Is it not enough that you should steal the wear of these things ? Must you light your fires by my beautiful stool ? "

Arachi replied philosophically and without passion : they might take his grand furnishings —which they did ; they might revile him in tones

and in language the most provocative—this also
they did ; but they could not take the noble hut
which their labours had built, because that was
against the law of the tribe ; nor could they
rob him of his faith in himself, because that
was contrary to the laws of nature—Arachi's
nature.

" My wife," he said to the weeping girl, " these
things happen. Now I think I am the victim of
Fate, therefore I propose changing all my gods.
Such as I have do not serve me, and, if you remember, I spent many hours in the forest with
my *bete*."

Arachi had thought of many possible contin-
gencies—as, for instance :

Sandi might relent, and appoint him to a great
chieftainship.

Or he might dig from the river-bed some such
treasure as U'fabi, the N'gombi man, did once
upon a time.

Arachi, entranced with this latter idea, went
one morning before sunrise to a place by the shore
and dug. He turned two spadefuls of earth before
an infinite weariness fell upon him, and he gave up
the search.

" For," he argued, " if treasure is buried in the
river-bed, it might as well be there as elsewhere.
And if it be not there, where may it be ? "

Arachi bore his misfortune with philosophy.
He sat in the bare and bleak interior of his hut,
and explained to his wife that the men who had
robbed him—as he said—hated him, and were

jealous of him because of his great powers, and that one day, when he was a great chief, he would borrow an army from his friends the N'gombi, and put fire to their houses.

Yes, indeed, he said "borrow," because it was his nature to think in loans.

His father-in-law came on the day following the deporting, expecting to save something from the wreckage on account of Korari's dowry. But he was very late.

"O son of shame!" he said bitterly. "Is it thus you repay for my priceless daughter? By Death! but you are a wicked man."

"Have no fear, fisherman," said Arachi loftily, "for I am a friend of Sandi, and be sure that he will do that for me which will place me high above common men. Even now I go to make a long palaver with him, and, when I return, you shall hear news of strange happenings."

Arachi was a most convincing man, possessing the powers of all great borrowers, and he convinced his father-in-law—a relation who, from the beginning of time, has always been the least open to conviction.

He left his wife, and she, poor woman, glad to be relieved of the presence of her loquacious husband, probably went to sleep.

At any rate, Arachi came to headquarters at a propitious moment for him. Headquarters at that moment was an armed camp at the junction of the Isisi and Ikeli rivers.

On the top of all his other troubles, Sanders

had the problem of a stranger who had arrived unbidden. His orderly came to him and told him that a man desired speech of him.

" What manner of man ? " asked Sanders, wearily.

" Master," said the orderly, " I have not seen a man like him before."

Sanders went out to inspect his visitor. The stranger rose and saluted, raising both hands, and the Commissioner looked him over. He was not of any of the tribes he knew, being without the face-cuts laterally descending either cheek. which mark the Bomongo. Neither was he tattooed on the forehead, like the people of the Little River.

" Where do you come from ? " asked Sanders, in Swaheli—which is the *lingua franca* of the continent —but the man shook his head.

So Sanders tried him again, this time in Bomongo, thinking, from his face-marks, that he must be a man of the Bokeri people. But he answered in a strange tongue.

" *Quel nom avez vous ?* " Sanders asked, and repeated the question in Portuguese. To this latter he responded, saying that he was a small chief of the Congo Angola, and that he had left his land to avoid slavery.

" Take him to the men's camp and feed him," said Sanders, and dismissed him from his mind.

Sanders had little time to bother about stray natives who might wander into his camp. He was engaged in searching for a gentleman who was

known as Abdul Hazim, a great rascal, trading guns
and powder contrary to the law.

"And," said Sanders to the captain of the
Houssas, "if I catch him he'll be sorry."

Abdul Hazim shared this view, so kept out of
Sanders's way to such purpose that, after a week's
further wanderings, Sanders returned to his headquarters.

Just about then he was dispirited, physically
low from the after-effects of fever, and mentally
disturbed.

Nothing went right with the Commissioner.
There had been a begging letter from head-quarters
concerning this same Abdul Hazim. He was in
no need of Houssa palavers, yet there must needs
come a free fight amongst these valiant soldier-men,
and, to crown all, two hours afterwards, the Houssa
skipper had gone to bed with a temperature of
104.6.

"Bring the swine here," said Sanders inele-
gantly, when the sergeant of Houssas reported
the fight. And there were marched before him the
strange man, who had come to him from the back-
lands, and a pugnacious soldier named Kano.

"Lord," said the Houssa, "by my god, who is,
I submit, greater than most gods, I am not to
blame. This Kaffir dog would not speak to me
when I spoke; also, he put his hands to my meat,
so I struck him."

"Is that all?" asked Sanders.

"That is all, lord."

"And did the stranger do no more than, in his

ignorance, touch your meat, and keep silence when you spoke ? "

" No more, lord."

Sanders leant back in his seat of justice and scowled horribly at the Houssa.

" If there is one thing more evident to me than another," he said slowly, " it is that a Houssa is a mighty person, a lord, a king. Now I sit here in justice, respecting neither kings, such as you be, nor slaves, such as this silent one. And I judge so, regarding the dignity of none, according to the law of the book. Is that so ? "

" That is so, lord."

" And it would seem that it is against the law to raise hand against any man, however much he offends you, the proper course being to make complaint according to the regulations of the service. Is that so ? "

" That is so, lord."

" Therefore you have broken the law. Is that truth ? "

" That is truth, lord."

" Go back to your lines, admitting this truth to your comrades, and let the Kaffir rest. For on the next occasion, for him that breaks the law, there will be breaking of skin. The palaver is finished."

The Houssa retired.

" And," said Sanders, retailing the matter to the convalescent officer next morning, " I consider that I showed more than ordinary self-restraint in not kicking both of them to the devil."

" You're a great man," said the Houssa officer. " You'll become a colonial-made gentleman one of these days, unless you're jolly careful."

Sanders passed in silence the Houssa's gibe at the Companionship of St. Michael and St. George, and, moreover, C.M.G.'s were not likely to come his way whilst Abdul Hazim was still at large.

He was in an unpleasant frame of mind when Arachi came swiftly in a borrowed canoe, paddled by four men whom he had engaged at an Isisi village, on a promise of payment which it was very unlikely he would ever be able to fulfil.

" Master," said Arachi solemnly, " I come desiring to serve your lordship, for I am too great a man for my village, and, if no chief, behold, I have a chief's thoughts."

" And a chief's hut," said Sanders dryly, " if all they tell me is true."

Arachi winced.

" Lord," he said humbly, " all things are known to you, and your eye goes forth like a chameleon's tongue to see round the corners."

Sanders passed over the unpleasant picture Arachi suggested.

" Arachi," he said, " it happens that you have come at a moment when you can serve me, for there is in my camp a strange man from a far-away land, who knows not this country, yet desires to cross it. Now, since you know the Angola tongue, you shall take him in your canoe to the edge of the Frenchi land, and there you shall put him on his way. And for this I will pay your paddlers.

And as for you, I will remember you in the day of your need."

It was not as Arachi could have wished, but it was something. The next day he departed importantly.

Before he left, Sanders gave him a word of advice.

" Go you, Arachi," he said, " by the Little Kusu River."

" Lord," said Arachi, " there is a shorter way by the creek of Still Waters. This goes to the Frenchi land, and is deep enough for our purpose."

" It is a short way and a long way," said Sanders grimly. " For there sits a certain Abdul Hazim who is a great buyer of men, and, because the Angola folk are wonderful gardeners, behold, the Arab is anxious to come by them. Go in peace."

" On my head," said Arachi, and took his leave.

It was rank bad luck that he should meet on his way two of his principal creditors. These, having some grievance in the matter of foodstuffs, advanced, desiring to do him an injury, but, on his earnest entreaties, postponed the performance of their solemn vows.

" It seems," said one of them, " that you are now Sandi's man, for though I do not believe anything you have told me, yet these paddlers do not lie."

" Nor this silent one," said Arachi, pointing to his charge proudly. " And because I alone in all the land can make palaver with him, Sandi has sent me on a mission to certain kings. These will give me presents, and on my return I will pay you what I owe, and much more for love."

They let him pass.

It may be said that Arachi, who lent " to none and believed no man," had no faith whatever in his lord's story. Who the silent Angola was, what was his mission, and why he had been chosen to guard the stranger, Arachi did not guess.

He would have found an easy way to understanding if he had believed all that Sanders had told him, but that was not Arachi's way.

On a night when the canoe was beached on an island, and the paddlers prepared the noble Arachi's food, the borrower questioned his charge.

" How does it happen, foreigner," he asked, " that my friend and neighbour, Sandi, asks me of my kindness to guide you to the French land ? "

" Patron," said the Angola man, " I am a stranger, and desire to escape from slavery. Also, there is a small Angola-Balulu tribe, which are of my people and faith, who dwell by the Frenchi tribe."

" What is your faith ? " asked Arachi.

" I believe in devils and ju-jus," said the Angola man simply, " especially one called Billimi, who has ten eyes and spits at snakes. Also, I hate the Arabi, that being part of my faith."

This gave Arachi food for thought, and some reason for astonishment that Sandi should have spoken the truth to him.

" What of this Abdul Arabi ? " he asked. " Now I think that Sandi lied to me when he said such an one buys men, for, if this be so, why does he not raid the Isisi? "

But the Angola man shook his head.

" These are matters too high for my understanding," he said. " Yet I know that he takes the Angola because they are great gardeners, and cunning in the pruning of trees."

Again Arachi had reason for thinking profoundly.

This Abdul, as he saw, must come to the Upper River for the people of the Lesser Akasava, who were also great gardeners. He would take no Isisi, because they were notoriously lazy, and moreover, died with exasperating readiness when transplanted to a foreign soil.

He continued his journey till he came to the place where he would have turned off had he taken a short cut to the French territory.

Here he left his paddlers and his guest, and made his way up the creek of Still Waters.

Half-a-day's paddling brought him to the camp of Abdul. The slaver's silent runners on the bank had kept pace with him, and when Arachi landed he was seized by men who sprang apparently from nowhere.

" Lead me to your master, O common men," said Arachi, " for I am a chief of the Isisi, and desire a secret palaver."

" If you are Isisi, and by your thinness and your boasting I see that you are," said his captor, " my lord Abdul will make easy work of you."

Abdul Hazim was short and stout, and a lover of happiness. Therefore he kept his camp in that condition of readiness which enabled him to leave quickly at the first sight of a white helmet or a Houssa's tarboosh.

For it would have brought no happiness to Abdul had Sanders come upon him.

Now, seated on a soft-hued carpet of silk before the door of his little tent, he eyed Arachi dubiously, and listened in silence while the man spoke of himself.

"Kaffir," he said, when the borrower had finished, "how do I know that you do not lie, or that you are not one of Sandi's spies? I think I should be very clever if I cut your throat."

Arachi explained at length why Abdul Hazim should not cut his throat.

"If you say this Angola man is near by, why should I not take him without payment?" asked the slaver.

"Because," said Arachi, "this foreigner is not the only man in the country, and because I have great influence with Sandi, and am beloved by all manner of people who trust me. I may bring many other men to your lordship."

Arachi returned to the camp, towing a small canoe with which the slaver had provided him.

He woke the Angola stranger from his sleep.

"Brother," he said, "here is a canoe with food. Now I tell you to paddle one day up this creek of Still Waters and there await my coming, for there are evil men about, and I fear for your safety."

The Angolan, simple man that he was, obeyed.

Half a day's journey up the creek Abdul's men were waiting.

Arachi set off for his own village that night, and in his canoe was such a store of cloth, of salt, and of brass rods as would delight any man's heart. Arachi came to his village singing a little song about himself.

In a year he had grown rich, for there were many ways of supplying the needs of an Arab slaver, and Abdul paid promptly.

Arachi worked single-handed, or, if he engaged paddlers, found them in obscure corners of the territories. He brought to Abdul many marketable properties, mostly young N'gombi women, who are fearful and easily cowed, and Sanders, scouring the country for the stout man with the fez, found him not.

*   *   *

"Lord Abdul," said Arachi, who met the slaver secretly one night near the Ikusi River, "Sandi and his soldiers have gone down to the Akasava for a killing palaver. Now I think we will do what you wish."

They were discussing an aspect of an adventure —the grandest adventure which Abdul had ever planned.

"Arachi," said Abdul, "I have made you a rich man. Now, I tell you that I can make you richer than any chief in this land."

"I shall be glad to hear of this," said Arachi.

" For though I am rich, yet I have borrowed many
things, and, it seems, I have so wonderful a mind
that I must live always in to-morrow."

" So I have heard," said the Arab. " For they
say of you that if you had the whole world you
would borrow the moon."

" That is my mystery," said Arachi modestly.
" For this reason I am a very notable man."

Then he sat down to listen in patience to the
great plan of Abdul Hazim. And it was a very
high plan, for there were two thousand Liberian
dollars at the back of it, and, for Arachi, payment
in kind.

At the moment of the conference, Sanders was
housed in the Ochori city making palaver with
Bosambo, the chief.

" Bosambo," said Sanders, " I have given you
these upper streams to your care. Yet Abdul
Hazim walks through the land without hurt, and
I think it is shame to you and to me."

" Master," said Bosambo, " it is a shameful
thing. Yet the streams hereabouts are so many,
and Abdul is a cunning man, and has spies. Also,
my people are afraid to offend him lest he ' chop '
them, or sell them into the interior."

Sanders nodded and rose to join the *Zaire.*

" Bosambo," he said, " this government put a
price upon this Abdul, even as a certain government
put a price upon you."

" What is his price, lord ? " asked Bosambo,
with an awakening of interest.

" One hundred pounds in silver," said Sanders.

" Lord," said Bosambo, " that is a good price."

Two days afterwards, when Arachi came to Bosambo, this chief was engaged in the purely domestic occupation of nursing his one small son.

" Greeting, Bosambo," said Arachi, " to you and to your beautiful son, who is noble in appearance and very quiet."

" Peace be to you, Arachi. I have nothing to lend you," said Bosambo.

" Lord," said Arachi loftily, " I am now a rich man—richer than chiefs—and I do not borrow."

" Ko, ko ! " said Bosambo, with polite incredulity.

" Bosambo," Arachi went on, " I came to you because I love you, and you are not a talking man, but rather a wise and silent one."

" All this I know, Arachi," said Bosambo cautiously. " And again I say to you that I lend no man anything."

The exasperated Arachi raised his patient eyes to heaven.

" Lord Bosambo," he said, in the tone of one hurt, " I came to tell you of that which I have found, and to ask your lordship to help me secure it. For in a certain place I have come across a great stock of ivory, such as the old kings buried against their need."

" Arachi," said Bosambo, of a sudden, " you tell me that you are rich. Now you are a little man and I am a chief, yet I am not rich."

" I have many friends," said Arachi, trembling with pride, " and they give me rods and salt."

" That is nothing," said Bosambo. " Now I

understand richness, for I have lived amongst white folk who laugh at rods and throw salt to dogs."

"Lord Bosambo," said the other eagerly, "I am rich also by white men's rule. Behold!"

From his waist pouch he took a handful of silver, and offered it in both hands for the chief's inspection.

Bosambo examined the money respectfully, turning each coin over gingerly.

"That is good riches," he said, and he breathed a little faster than was his wont. "And it is new, being bright. Also the devil marks, which you do not understand, are as they should be."

The gratified Arachi shoved his money back into his pouch. Bosambo sat in meditative silence, his face impassive.

"And you will take me, Arachi, to the place of buried treasure?" he asked slowly. "Ko! you are a generous man, for I do not know why you should share with me, knowing that I once beat you."

Bosambo put the child down gently. These kings' stores were traditional. Many had been found, and it was the dream of every properly constituted man to unearth such.

Yet Bosambo was not impressed, being in his heart sceptical.

"Arachi," he said, "I believe that you are a liar! Yet I would see this store, and, if it be near by, will see with my own eyes."

It was one day's journey, according to Arachi.

" You shall tell me where this place is," said Bosambo.

Arachi hesitated.

" Lord, how do I not know that you will not go and take this store ? " he asked.

Bosambo regarded him sternly.

" Am I not an honest man ? " he asked. " Do not the people from one end of the world to the other swear by the name of Bosambo ? "

" No," said Arachi truthfully.

Yet he told of the place. It was by the River of Shadows, near the Crocodile Pool Where-the-Floods Had-Changed-The-Land.

Bosambo went to his hut to make preparations for the journey.

Behind his house, in a big grass cage, were many little pigeons. He laboriously wrote in his vile Arabic a laconic message, and attached it to the leg of a pigeon.

To make absolutely sure, for Bosambo left nothing to chance, he sent away a canoe secretly that night for a certain destination.

" And this you shall say to Sandi," said the chief to his trusted messenger, " that Arachi is rich with the richness of silver, and that silver has the devil marks of Zanzibar—being the home of all traders, as your lordship knows."

Next day, at dawn, Bosambo and his guide departed. They paddled throughout the day, taking the smaller stream that drained the eastern side of the river, and at night they camped at a place called Bolulu, which means " the changed land."

They rose with the daylight to resume their journey. But it was unnecessary, for, in the darkness before the dawn, Abdul Hazim had surrounded the camp, and, at the persuasive muzzle of a Snider rifle, Bosambo accompanied his captors ten minutes' journey into the wood where Abdul awaited him.

The slaver, sitting before the door of his tent on his silken carpet, greeted his captive in the Ochori dialect. Bosambo replied in Arabic

"Ho, Bosambo!" said Abdul. "Do you know me?"

"Sheikh," said Bosambo, "I would know you in hell, for you are the man whose head my master desires."

"Bosambo," said Abdul calmly, "your head is more valuable, so they say, for the Liberians will put it upon a pole, and pay me riches for my enterprise."

Bosambo laughed softly. "Let the palaver finish," he said, "I am ready to go."

They brought him to the river again, tied him to a pole, and laid him in the bottom of a canoe, Arachi guarding him.

Bosambo, looking up, saw the borrower squatting on guard.

"Arachi," he said, "if you untie my hands, it shall go easy with you."

"If I untie your hands," said Arachi frankly, "I am both a fool and a dead man, and neither of these conditions is desirable."

"To every man," quoth Bosambo, "there is

an easy kill somewhere,* and, if he misses this, all kills are difficult."

Four big canoes composed the waterway caravan. Abdul was in the largest with his soldiers, and led the van.

They moved quickly down the tiny stream, which broadened as it neared the river.

Then Abdul's headman suddenly gasped.

" Look ! " he whispered.

The slaver turned his head.

Behind them, paddling leisurely, came four canoes, and each was filled with armed men.

" Quickly," said Abdul, and the paddlers stroked furiously, then stopped.

Ahead was the *Zaire,* a trim, white steamer, alive with Houssas.

" It is God's will," said Abdul. " These things are ordained."

He said no more until he stood before Sanders, and the Commissioner was not especially communicative.

" What will you do with me ? " asked Abdul.

" I will tell you when I have seen your stores," said Sanders. " If I find rifles such as the foolish Lobolo people buy, I shall hang you according to law."

The Arab looked at the shaking Arachi. The borrower's knees wobbled fearfully.

" I see," said Abdul thoughtfully, " that this man whom I made rich has betrayed me."

If he had hurried or moved jerkily Sanders would

* The native equivalent for " opportunity knocks," etc.

have prevented the act; but the Arab searched calmly in the fold of his *bournous* as though seeking a cigarette.

His hand came out, and with it a curved knife.

Then he struck quickly, and Arachi went blubbering to the deck, a dying man.

" Borrower," said the Arab, and he spoke from the centre of six Houssas who were chaining him, so that he was hidden from the sobbing figure on the floor, " I think you have borrowed that which you can at last repay. For it is written in the Sura of the Djinn that from him who takes a life, let his life be taken, that he may make full repayment."

CHAPTER II

THE TAX RESISTERS

SANDERS took nothing for granted when he accounted for native peoples. These tribes of his possessed an infinite capacity for unexpectedness—therein lay at once their danger and their charm. For one could neither despair at their sin nor grow too confidently elated at their virtue, knowing that the sun which went down on the naughtiness of the one and the dovelike placidity of the other, might rise on the smouldering sacrificial fires in the streets of the blessed village, and reveal the folk of the incorrigible sitting at the doors of their huts, dust on head, hands outspread in an agony of penitence.

Yet it seemed that the people of Kiko were models of deportment, thrift, and intelligence, and that the gods had given them beautiful natures.

Kiko, a district of the Lower Isisi, is separated from all other tribes and people by the Kiko on the one side, the Isisi River on the other, and on the third by clumps of forest land set at irregular intervals in the Great Marsh.

Kiko proper stretches from the marsh to the tongue

of land at the confluence of the Kiko and Isisi, in the shape of an irregular triangle.

To the eastward, across the Kiko River, are the unruly N'gombi tribes; to the westward, on the farther bank of the big river, are the Akasava; and the Kiko people enjoy an immunity from sudden attack, which is due in part to its geographical position, and in part to the remorseless activities of Mr. Commissioner Sanders.

Once upon a time a king of the N'gombi called his headmen and chiefs together to a great palaver.

"It seems to me," he said, "that we are children. For our crops have failed because of the floods, and the thieving Ochori have driven the game into their own country. Now, across the river are the Kiko people, and they have reaped an oat harvest; also, there is game in plenty. Must we sit and starve whilst the Kiko swell with food?"

A fair question, though the facts were not exactly stated, for the N'gombi were lazy, and had sown late; also the game was in their forest for the searching, but, as the saying is, "The N'gombi hunts from his bed and seeks only cooked meats."

One night the N'gombi stole across the river and fell upon Kiko city, establishing themselves masters of the country.

There was a great palaver, which was attended by the chief and headman of the Kiko.

"Henceforward," said the N'gombi king—Tigilini was his name—"you are as slaves to my people, and if you are gentle and good and work in the fields you shall have one-half of all you produce,

B

for I am a just man, and very merciful. But if you rebel, I will take you for my sport."

Lest any misunderstanding should exist, he took the first malcontent, who was a petty chief of a border village, and performed his programme.

This man had refused tribute, and was led, with roped hands, before the king, all headmen having been summoned to witness the happening.

The rebel was bound with his hands behind him, and was ordered to kneel. A young sapling was bent over, and one end of a native rope was fixed to its topmost branches, and the other about his neck. The tree was slowly released till the head of the offender was held taut.

"Now!" said the king, and his executioner struck off the head, which was flung fifty yards by the released sapling.

It fell at the feet of Mr. Commissioner Sanders, who, with twenty-five Houssas and a machine gun, had just landed from the *Zaire*.

Sanders was annoyed; he had travelled three days and four nights with little sleep, and he had a touch of fever, which made him irritable.

He walked into the village and interrupted an eloquent address on the obligations of the conquered, which the N'gombi thief thought it opportune to deliver.

He stopped half-way through his speech, and lost a great deal of interest in the proceedings as the crowd divided to allow of Sanders's approach.

"Lord," said Tigilini, that quick and subtle man, "you have come at a proper time, for these people were in rebellion against your lordship, and I have subdued them. Therefore, master, give me rewards as you gave to Bosambo of the Ochori."

Sanders gave nothing save a brief order, and his Houssas formed a half circle about the hut of the king—Tigilini watching the manœuvre with some apprehension.

"If," he said graciously. "I have done anything which your lordship thinks I should not have done, or taken that which I should not have taken, I will undo and restore."

Sanders, hands on hips, regarded him dispassionately.

"There is a body." He pointed to the stained and huddled thing on the ground. "There, by the path, is a head. Now, you shall put the head to that body and restore life."

"That I cannot do," said the king nervously, "for I am no ju-ju."

Sanders spoke two words in Arabic, and Tigilini was seized.

They carried the king away, and no man ever saw his face again, and it is a legend that Tigilini, the king, is everlastingly chained to the hind leg of M'shimba M'shamba, the green devil of the Akasava. If the truth be told, Tigilini went no nearer to perdition than the convict prison at Sierra Leone, but the legend is not without its value as a deterrent to ambitious chiefs.

Sanders superintended the evacuation of the Kiko, watched the crestfallen N'gombi retire to their own lands, and set up a new king without fuss or ceremony. And the smooth life of the Kiko people ran pleasantly as before.

They tilled the ground and bred goats and caught fish. From the marsh forest, which was their backland, they gathered rubber and copal, and this they carried by canoe to the mouth of the river and sold.

So they came to be rich, and even the common people could afford three wives.

Sanders was very wise in the psychology of native wealth. He knew that people who grew rich in corn were dangerous, because corn is an irresponsible form of property, and had no ramifications to hold in check the warlike spirit of its possessors.

He knew, too, that wealth in goats, in cloth, in brass rods, and in land was a factor for peace, because possessions which cannot be eaten are ever a steadying influence in communal life.

Sanders was a wise man. He was governed by certain hard and fast rules, and though he was well aware that failure in any respect to grapple with a situation would bring him a reprimand, either because he had not acted according to the strict letter of the law, or because he " had not used his discretion " in going outside that same inflexible code, he took responsibility without fear.

It was left to his discretion as to what part of the burden of taxation individual tribes should bear, and on behalf of his government he took his full share of the Kiko surplus, adjusting his demands according to the measure of the tribe's prosperity.

Three years after the enterprising incursion of the N'gombi, he came to the Kiko country on his half-yearly visit.

In the palaver house of the city he listened to complaints, as was his custom.

He sat from dawn till eight o'clock in the morning, and after the tenth complaint he turned to the chief of the Kiko, who sat at his side.

"Chief," he said, with that air of bland innocence which would have made men used to his ways shake in their tracks, "I observe that all men say one thing to me—that they are poor. Now this is not the truth."

"I am in your hands," said the chief diplomatically; "also my people, and they will pay taxation though they starve."

Sanders saw things in a new light.

"It seems," he said, addressing the serried ranks of people who squatted about, "that there is discontent in your stomachs because I ask you for your taxes. We will have a palaver on this."

He sat down, and a grey old headman, a notorious litigant and a league-long speaker, rose up.

"Lord," he said dramatically, "justice!"

"Kwai!" cried the people in chorus.

The murmur, deep-chested and unanimous, made a low, rumbling sound like the roll of a drum.

"Justice!" said the headman. "For you, Sandi, are very cruel and harsh. You take and take and give us nothing, and the people cry out in pain."

He paused, and Sanders nodded.

"Go on," he said.

"Corn and fish, gum and rubber, we give you," said the spokesman; "and when we ask whither goes this money, you point to the puc-a-puc* and your soldiers, and behold we are mocked. For your puc-a-puc comes only to take our taxes, and your soldiers to force us to pay."

Again the applauding murmur rolled.

"So we have had a palaver," said the headman, "and this we have said among ourselves: 'Let Sandi remit one-half our taxes; these we will bring in our canoes to the Village-by-the-Big-Water, for we are honest men, and let Sandi keep his soldiers and his puc-a-puc for the folk of the Isisi and the Akasava and the N'gombi, for these are turbulent and wicked people."

"Kwai!"

It was evidently a popular movement, and Sanders smiled behind his hand.

"As for us," said the headman, "we are peace able folk, and live comfortably with all nations, and if any demand of us that we shall pay tribute, behold it will be better to give freely than to pay these taxes."

Sanders listened in silence, then he turned to the chief.

"It shall be as you wish," he said, "and I will remit one half of your taxation—the palaver is finished."

* Steamer.

He went on board the *Zaire* that night and lay awake listening to the castanets of the dancing women—the Kiko made merry to celebrate the triumph of their diplomacy.

Sanders left next day for the Isisi, having no doubt in his mind that the news of his concession had preceded him. So it proved, for at Lukalili no sooner had he taken his place in the speech-house than the chief opened the proceedings.

"Lord Sandi," he began, "we are poor men, and our people cry out against taxation. Now, lord, we have thought largely on this matter, and this say the people : 'If your lordship would remit one-half our taxes we should be happy, for this puc-a-puc '——"

Sanders waved him down.

"Chiefs and people," he said, "I am patient, because I love you. But talk to me more about taxation and about puc-a-pucs, and I will find a new chief for me, and you will wish that you had never been born."

After that Sanders had no further trouble.

He came to the Ochori, and found Bosambo, wholly engrossed with his new baby, but ripe for action.

"Bosambo," said the Commissioner, after he had gingerly held the new-comer and bestowed his natal present, "I have a story to tell you."

He told his story, and Bosambo found it vastly entertaining.

Five days later, when Sanders was on his way home, Bosambo with ten picked men for paddlers, came sweeping up the river, and beached at Kiko city.

He was greeted effusively ; a feast was prepared for him, the chief's best hut was swept clean.

" Lord Bosambo," said the Kiko chief, when the meal was finished, " I shall have a sore heart this night when you are gone."

" I am a kind man," said Bosambo, " so I will not go to-night, for the thought of your sorrow would keep sleep from my eyes."

" Lord," said the chief hastily, " I am not used to sorrow, and, moreover, I shall sleep heavily, and it would be shameful if I kept you from your people, who sigh like hungry men for your return."

" That is true," said Bosambo, " yet I will stay this night, because my heart is full of pleasant thoughts for you."

" If you left to-night," said the embarrassed chief, " I would give you a present of two goats."

" Goats," said Bosambo, " I do not eat, being of a certain religious faith——"

" Salt I will give you also," said the chief.

" I stay to-night," said Bosambo emphatically ; " to-morrow I will consider the matter."

The next morning Bosambo went to bathe in the river, and returned to see the chief of the Kiko squatting before the door of his hut, vastly glum.

" Ho, Cetomati ! " greeted Bosambo, " I have news which will gladden your heart."

A gleam of hope shone in the chief's eye.

" Does my brother go so soon ? " he asked pointedly.

" Chief," said Bosambo acidly, " if that be good news to you, I go. And woe to you and your people, for I am a proud man, and my people are also proud. Likewise, they are notoriously vengeful."

The Kiko king rose in agitation.

" Lord," he said humbly, " my words are twisted, for, behold, all this night I have spent mourning in fear of losing your lordship. Now, tell me your good news that I may rejoice with you."

But Bosambo was frowning terribly, and was not appeased for some time.

" This is my news, O king ! " he said. " Whilst I bathed I beheld, far away, certain Ochori canoes, and I think they bring my councillors. If this be so, I may stay with you for a long time—rejoice ! "

The Kiko chief groaned.

He groaned more when the canoes arrived bringing reinforcements to Bosambo—ten lusty fighting men, terribly tall and muscular.

He groaned undisguisedly when the morrow brought another ten, and the evening some twenty more.

There are sayings on the river which are uncomplimentary to the appetites of the Ochori.

Thus : " Men eat to live fat, but the Ochori live to eat." And : " One field of corn will feed a village for a year, ten goats for a month, and an Ochori for a day."

Certainly Bosambo's followers were excellent trenchermen. They ate and they ate and they ate; from dawn till star time they alternated between the preparation of meals and their disposal.

The simple folk of the Kiko stood in a wondering circle about them and watched in amazement as their good food vanished.

"I see we shall starve when the rains come," said the chief in despair.

He sent an urgent canoe to Sanders, but Sanders was without sympathy.

"Go to your master," he said to the envoy, "telling him that all these things are his palaver. If he does not desire the guests of his house, let him turn them away, for the land is his, and he is chief."

Cold comfort for Cetomati this, for the Ochori sat in the best huts, eating the best foods, finding the best places at the dance-fires.

The king called a secret palaver of his headmen.

"These miserable Ochori thieves ruin us," he said. "Are we men or dogs? Now, I tell you, my people and councillors, that to-morrow I send Bosambo and his robbers away, though 1 die for it!"

"Kwai!" said the councillors in unison.

"Lord," said one, "in the times of *cala-cala* the Kiko folk were very fierce and bloody; perchance if we rouse the people with our eloquence they are still fierce and bloody."

The king looked dubious.

"I do not think" he said, "that the Kiko people are as fierce and bloody as at one time, for we have had many fat years. What I know, O friend, is that the Ochori are very fierce indeed, and Bosambo has killed many men."

He screwed up his courage through the night, and in the morning put it to the test.

Bosambo, in his most lordly way, had ordered a big hunting, and he and his men were assembling in the village street when the king and his councillors approached.

"Lord," said the king mildly, "I have that within me which I must tell."

"Say on," said Bosambo.

"Now, I love you, Bosambo," said the chief, "and the thought that I must speed you on your way—with presents—is very sad to me."

"More sad to me," said Bosambo ominously.

"Yet lord," said the desperate chief, "I must, for my people are very fierce with me that I keep you so long within our borders. Likewise, there is much sickness, and I fear lest you and your beautiful men also become sick, and die."

"Only one man in all the world, chief," said Bosambo, speaking with deliberation, "has ever put such shame upon me—and, king, that man— where is he?"

The king of the Kiko did not say, because he did not know. He could guess—oh, very well he could guess! —and Bosambo's next words justified his guesswork.

"He is dead," said Bosambo solemnly. "I will not say how he died, lest you think I am a boastful one, or whose hand struck him down, for fear you think vainly—nor as to the manner of his dying, for that would give you sorrow!"

"Bosambo," said the agitated chief of the Kiko, "these are evil words——"

"I say no evil words," said Bosambo, "for I am, as you know, the brother-in-law of Sandi, and it would give him great grief. I say nothing, O little king!"

With a lofty wave of his hand he strode away, and, gathering his men together, he marched them to the beach.

It was in vain that the chief of the Kiko had stored food in enormous quantities and presents in each canoe, that bags of salt were evenly distributed amongst the paddlers.

Bosambo, it is true, did not throw them back upon the shore, but he openly and visibly scorned them. The king, standing first on one foot and then on the other, in his anxiety and embarrassment, strove to give the parting something of a genial character, but Bosambo was silent, forbidding, and immensely gloomy.

"Lord," said the chief, "when shall my heart again be gladdened at the sight of your pretty face?"

"Who knows?" said Bosambo mysteriously. "Who can tell when I come, or my friends! For many men love me—Isisi, N'gombi, Akasava, Bongindi, and the Bush people."

He stepped daintily into his canoe.

"I tell you," he said, wagging a solemn forefinger, "that whatever comes to you, it is no palaver of mine; whoever steals quietly upon you in the night, it will not be Bosambo—I call all men to witness this saying."

And with this he went.

There was a palaver that night, where all men spoke at once, and the Kiko king did not more than bite his nails nervously. It was certain that attack would come.

"Let us meet them boldly," said the one who had beforetime rendered such advice. "For in times of *cala-cala* the Kiko folk were fierce and bloody people."

Whatever they might have been once, there was no spirit of adventure abroad then, and many voices united to call the genius who had suggested defiance a fool and worse.

All night long the Kiko stood a nation in arms.

Once the hooting of a bird sent them scampering to their huts with howls of fear; once a wandering buffalo came upon a quaking picket and scattered it. Night after night the fearful Kiko kept guard, sleeping as they could by day.

They saw no enemy; the suspense was worse than the vision of armed warriors. A messenger went to Sanders about the fears and apprehensions of the people, but Sanders was callous.

"If any people attack you, I will come with my soldiers, and for every man of you who dies, I will kill one of your enemies."

"Lord," said the messenger, none other than the king's son, "if we are dead, we care little who lives or dies. Now, I ask you, master, to send your soldiers with me, for our people are tired and timid."

"Be content," said Sanders, "that I have remitted your taxation—the palaver is finished."

The messenger returned to his dismal nation—
Sanders at the time was never more than a day's
journey from the Kiko—and a sick and weary
people sat down in despair to await the realisation
of their fears.

They might have waited throughout all eternity,
for Bosambo was back in his own city, and had
almost forgotten them, and Isisi and the Akasava,
regarding them for some reason as Sanders' *urglebes*,
would have no more thought of attacking them
than they would have considered the possibility
of attacking Sanders ; and as for the N'gombi,
they had had their lesson.

Thus matters stood when the Lulungo people,
who live three days beyond the Akasava, came
down the river looking for loot and trouble.

The Lulungo people are an unlovable race ;
" a crabbed, bitter, and a beastly people," Sanders
once described them in his wrath.

For two years the Lulungo folk had lain quiet,
then, like foraging and hungry dogs, they took the
river trail—six canoes daubed with mud and rushes.

They found hospitality of a kind in the fishing
villages, for the peaceable souls who lived therein
fled at the first news of the visitation.

They came past the Ochori warily keeping to
midstream. Time was when the Ochori would
have supplied them with all their requirements,
but nowadays these men of Bosambo's snapped
viciously.

" None the less," said Gomora, titular chief
of the Lulungo, to his headmen, " since we be so

strong the Ochori will not oppose us—let two canoes paddle to land."

The long boats were detached from the fleet and headed for the beach. A shower of arrows fell short of them, and they turned back.

The Isisi country they passed, the Akasava they gave the widest of berths to, for the Lulungo folk are rather cruel than brave, better assassins than fighting men, more willing to kill coldly than in hot blood.

They went lurching down the river, seizing such loot as the unprotected villages gave them.

It was a profitless expedition.

" Now we will go to Kiko," said Gomora ; " for these people are very rich, and, moreover, they are fearful. Speak to my people, and say that there shall be no killing, for that devil Sandi hates us, and he will incite the tribes against us, as he did in the days of my father "

They waited till night had fallen, and then, under the shadow of the river bank, they moved silently upon their prey.

" We will frighten them," confided Gomora ; " and they will give us what we ask ; then we will make them swear by Iwa that they will not speak to Sandi—it will be simple."

The Lulungo knew the Kiko folk too well, and they landed at a convenient place, making their way through the strip of forest without the display of caution which such a manœuvre would have necessitated had it been employed against a more warlike nation.

＊　　　＊　　　＊　　　＊

Sanders, hurrying down stream, his guns swung out and shotted for action, his armed Houssas sitting in the bow of the steamer, met two canoes, unmistakably Lulungo.

He circled and captured them. In one was Gomora, a little weak from loss of blood, but more bewildered.

"Lord," he said bitterly, "all this world is changed since you have come ; once the Ochori were meat for me and my people, being very timorous. Then by certain magic they became fierce fighters. And now, lord, the Kiko folk, who, up and down the river, are known for their gentleness, have become like devils."

Sanders waited, and the chief went on :

"Last night we came to the Kiko, desiring to rest with them, and in the dark of the forest they fell upon us, with great screaming ; and, behold ! of ten canoes these men are all I have left, for the Kiko were waiting for our coming."

He looked earnestly at Sanders.

"Tell me, lord," he said, "what magic do white men use to make warriors from cowards ? "

"That is not for your knowing," said Sanders diplomatically ; "yet you should put this amongst the sayings of your people, ' Every rat fights in his hole, and fear is more fierce than hate.' "

He went on to Kiko city, arriving in time to check an expedition, for the Kiko, filled with arrogance at their own powers, were assembling an army to attack the Ochori.

"Often have I told," said the chief, trembling

with pride, " that the Kiko were terrible and bloody—now, lord, behold ! In the night we slew our oppressors, for the spirit of our fathers returned to us, and our enemies could not check us."

" Excellent ! " said Sanders in the vernacular. " Now I see an end to all taxation palaver, for, truly, you do not desire my soldiers nor the puc-a-puc.   Yet, lest the Lulungo folk return—for they are as many as the sands of the river—I will send fighting men to help you."

" Lord you are as our father and mother," said the gratified chief.

" Therefore I will prevail upon Bosambo, whose heart is now sore against you, to come with his fighting tribes to sit awhile at your city."

The chief's face worked convulsively : he was as one swallowing a noxious draught.

" Lord," he said, speaking under stress of emotion, " we are a poor people, yet we may pay your lord-ship full taxes, for in the end I think it would be cheaper than Bosambo and his hungry devils."

" So I think ! " said Sanders.

CHAPTER III

THE RISE OF THE EMPEROR

TOBOLAKA, the king of the Isisi, was appointed for his virtues, being a Christian and a Bachelor of Arts.

For a time he ruled his country wisely and might have died full of honour, but his enthusiasm got the better of him.

For Tobolaka had been taken to America when a boy by an enthusiastic Baptist, had been educated at a college and had lectured in America and England. He wrote passable Latin verse, so I am told ; was a fluent exponent of the Free Silver Policy of Mr. Bryan, and wore patent leather shoes with broad silk laces.

In London he attracted the attention of a callow Under-Secretary of State for the Colonies, and this Under-Secretary was a nephew of the Prime Minister, cousin of the Minister of War, and son-in-law of the Lord Chancellor, so he had a pull which most Under-Secretaries do not ordinarily possess.

" Mr. Tobolaka," said the Under-Secretary, " what are your plans ? "

Mr. Tobolaka was a little restrained.

" I feel, Mr. Cardow," he said, " that my duties

48

lie in my land—no, I do not mean that I have any
call to missionary work, but rather to administra-
tion. I am, as you know of the Isisi people—
we are a pure Bantu stock, as far as legend supports
that contention—and I have often thought, remembering that the Isisi are the dominant race, that
there are exceptional opportunities for an agglomera-
tion of interests ; in fact——"

" A splendid idea—a great idea ! " said the
enthusiastic Under-Secretary.

Now it happened that this young Mr. Cardow
had sought for years for some scheme which he
might further to his advantage. He greatly desired,
after the fashion of all budding Parliamentarians,
to be associated with a movement which would
bring kudos and advertisement in its train, and
which would earn for him the approval or the
condemnation of the Press, according to the shade
of particular opinion which the particular newspapers
represented.

So in the silence of his room in Whitehall Court,
he evolved a grand plan which he submitted to
his chief. That great man promised to read it
on a given day, and was dismayed when he found
himself confronted with forty folios of typewritten
matter at the very moment when he was hurrying
to catch the 10.35 to the Cotswold Golf Links.

" I will read it in the train," he said.

He crammed the manuscript into his bag and
forgot all about it ; on his return to town he discovered that by some mischance he had left the
great scheme behind.

Nevertheless, being a politician and resourceful, he wrote to his subordinate.

"DEAR CARDOW,—I have read your valuable document with more than ordinary interest. I think it is an excellent idea,"—he knew it was an idea because Cardow had told him so—"but I see many difficulties. Mail me another copy. I should like to send it to a friend of mine who would give me an expert opinion."

It was a wily letter, but indiscreet, for on the strength of that letter the Under-Secretary enlisted the sympathies and practical help of his chief's colleagues.

"Here we have a native and an educated native," he said impressively, "who is patriotic, intelligent, resourceful. It is a unique opportunity—a splendid opportunity. Let him go back to his country and get the threads together."

The conversation occurred in the Prime Minister's room, and there were present three Ministers of the Crown, including a Home Secretary, who was frankly bored, because he had a scheme of his own, and would much rather have discussed his Artisans' Tenement (19—) Bill.

"Isn't there a Commissioner Sanders in that part of the world?" he asked languidly. "I seem to remember some such name. And isn't there likely to be trouble with the minor chiefs if you set up a sort of Central African Emperor?"

"That can be overcome." said the sanguine

Cardow. " As for Sanders, I expect him to help.
A dynasty established on the Isisi River might
end all the troubles we have had there."

" It might end other things," said the impatient
Home Secretary. " Now about this Tenement
Bill. I think we ought to accept Cronk's amend-
ment—er——"

A few weeks later Mr. Tobolaka was summoned
to Whitehall Court.

" I think, Mr. Tobolaka," said Cardow complacently, " I have arranged for a trial of our
plan. The Government has agreed—after a tough
fight with the permanent officials, I admit—to
establish you on the Isisi as King and Overlord
of the Isisi, Ochori, N'gombi, and Akasava. They
will vote you a yearly allowance, and will build
a house in Isisi city for you. You will find Mr.
Sanders—er—difficult, but you must have a great
deal of patience."

" Sir," said Mr. Tobolaka, speaking under stress
of profound emotion, " I'm e-eternally obliged.
You've been real good to me, and I guess I'll make
good."

Between the date of Tobolaka's sailing and his
arrival Sanders ordered a palaver of all chiefs,
and they came to meet him in the city of the
Isisi.

" Chiefs and headmen," said Sanders, " you
know that many moons ago the Isisi people rose
in an evil moment and made sacrifice contrary
to the law. So I came with my soldiers and took
away the king to the Village of Irons, where he

now sits. Because the Isisi are foolish people, my Government sets up a new king, who is Tobolaka, son of Yoka'n'kema, son of Ichulomo, the son of Tibilino."

" Lord," gasped an Isisi headman, " this Tobolaka I remember. The God-folk took him away to their own land, where he learnt to be white."

" Yet I promise you that he is black," said Sanders drily, " and will be blacker. Also, chiefs of the Ochori, N'gombi, and Akasava, this new king will rule you, being paramount king of these parts, and you shall bring him presents and tribute according to custom."

There was an ominous silence.

Then O'kara, the chief of the Akasava, an old and arrogant man, spoke :

" Lord," he said, " many things have I learnt, such as mysteries and devil magic, yet I have not learnt in my life that the Akasava pay tribute to the Isisi, for, lord, in the year of the Floods, the Akasava fought with the Isisi and made them run ; also, in the year of the Elephants, we defeated the Isisi on land and water, and would have sat down in their city if your lordship had not come with guns and soldiers and tempted us to go home."

The Akasava headmen murmured their approval.

" Alas," said the chief of the N'gombi, " we people of the N'gombi are fierce men, and often have we made the Isisi tremble by our mighty shouts. Now I should be ashamed to bring tribute to Tobolaka."

The palaver waited for Bosambo of the Ochori

to speak, but he was silent, for he had not grasped the bias of the Commissioner's mind. Other men spoke at length, taking their cue from their chiefs, but the men of the Ochori said nothing.

"For how was I to speak?" said Bosambo, after the palaver. "No man knows how your lordship thinks."

"You have ears," said Sanders, a little irritated.

"They are large," admitted Bosambo, "so large that they hear your beautiful voice, but not so long that they hear your lordship's loving thoughts."

Sanders's thoughts were by no means loving, and they diminished in beauty day by day as the ship which carried Tobolaka to his empire drew nearer.

Sanders did not go down to the beach to meet him; he awaited his coming on the verandah of the residency, and when Tobolaka arrived, clad from head to foot in spotless white, with a helmet of exact colonial pattern on his head, Sanders swore fluently at all interfering and experimenting Governments.

"Mr. Sanders, I presume?" said Tobolaka in English, and extended his hand.

"Chief," said Sanders in the Isisi tongue, "you know that I am Sandi, so do not talk like a monkey; speak rather in the language of your people, and I will understand you better—also you will understand me."

It so happened that Tobolaka had prepared a dignified little speech in the course of which he intended congratulating Sanders on the prosperity of the country, assuring him of wholehearted co-operation, and winding up with an expression of his wishes that harmonious relation should exist between himself and the State.

It was founded on a similar speech delivered by King Peter of Servia on his assuming the crown. But, unfortunately, it was in English, and the nearest Isisi equivalent for congratulation is an idiomatic phrase which literally means, "Highman-look-kindly-on-dog-slave-who-lies-at-feet." And this, thought Tobolaka, would never do at all, for he had come to put the Commissioner in his place.

Sanders condescended to talk English later when Tobolaka was discussing Cabinet Ministers.

"I shall—at the Premier's request—endeavour to establish district councils," he said. "I think it is possible to bring the native to a realisation of his responsibility. As Cicero said——"

"Do not bother about Cicero," said Sanders coldly. "It is not what Cicero said, but what Bosambo will say: there are philosophers on this river who could lose the ancients."

Tobolaka, in a canoe sent for him by the Isisi folk, went to his new home. He hinted broadly that a state entrance in the *Zaire* would be more in keeping with the occasion.

"And a ten-gun salute, I suppose!" snarled Sanders in Isisi. "Get to your land, chief, before I lose my patience, for I am in no mood to palaver with you."

Tobolaka stopped long enough at headquarters to write privately to the admirable Mr. Cardow, complaining that he had received " scant courtesy " at the hands of the Commissioner. He had shown " deplorable antagonism." The letter concluded with respectful wishes regarding Mr. Cardow's health, and there was a postscript, significant and ominous to the effect that the writer hoped to cement the good feeling which already existed between Great Britain and the United States of America by means which he did not disclose.

The excellent Mr. Cardow was frankly puzzled by the cryptic postscript, but was too much occupied with a successful vote of censure on the Government which had turned him into the cold shades of Opposition to trouble to reply.

Tobolaka came to his city and was accorded a rapturous welcome by a people who were prepared at any given hour of the day or night to jubilate over anything which meant dances and feasts.

He sat in the palaver house in his white duck suit and his white helmet, with a cavalry sword (this Sanders had not seen) between his knees, his white-gloved hands resting on the hilt.

And he spoke to the people in Isisi, which they understood, and in English, which they did not understand, but thought wonderful. He also recited as much of the " Iliad " as he could remember, and then, triumphant and a little hoarse, he was led to the big hut of chieftainship, and was waited upon by young girls who danced for his amusement.

Sanders heard of these things and more.

He learnt that the Isisi were to be ruled in European fashion. To Tobolaka came Cala, a sycophantic old headman from the village of Toroli, with soft and oily words. Him the king promoted to be Minister of Justice, though he was a notorious thief. Mijilini, the fisher chief, Tobolaka made his Minister of War ; he had a Home Secretary, a Minister of Agriculture, and a Fishery Commissioner.

Sanders, steaming up-river, was met by the canoe of Limibolo, the Akasava man, and his canoe was decorated with clothes and spears as for a wedding.

" Lord," said the dignified Limibolo, " I go to my village to hold a palaver, for my lord the king has called me by a certain name which I do not understand, but it has to do with the hanging of evil men, and, by Iwa ! I know two men in my village who owe me salt, and they shall hang at once, by Death ! "

" Then will I come and you shall hang also ! " said Sanders cheerlessly. " Be sure of that."

It transpired that the light-hearted Limibolo had been created sheriff.

Tobolaka was on the point of raising an army for his dignity, when Sanders came upon the scene.

He arrived without warning, and Tobolaka had no opportunity for receiving him in the state which the king felt was due equally to himself and to the representative of Government.

But he had ample time to come to the beach to greet the Commissioner according to custom.

Instead, he remained before his hut and sent his minister in attendance, the ignoble Cala.

" O Cala ! " said Sanders as he stepped ashore across the *Zaire's* narrow gangway, " what are you in this land ? "

" Lord," said Cala, " I am a great catcher of thieves by order of our lord ; also, I check evil in every place."

" O Ko ! " said Sanders offensively, " now since you are the biggest thief of all, I think you had best catch yourself before I catch you."

He walked through Isisi city.

The king had been busy. Rough boards had been erected at every street corner.

There was a " Downing Street," a " Fifth Avenue," a " Sacramento Street," a " Piccadilly," and a " Broadway."

" These," explained Cala, " are certain devil marks which my king has put up to warn witches and spirits, and they have much virtue, for, lord, my son, who was troubled with pains in his stomach, as there "—he indicated " Broadway "—" and the pain left him."

" It would," said Sanders.

Tobolaka rose from his throne and offered his hand.

" I am sorry, Mr. Sanders," he began, " you did not give us notice of your coming."

" When I come again, Tobolaka," said Sanders, staring with his passionate grey eyes at the white-clad figure. " you shall come to the beach to meet me, for that is the custom."

" But not the law," smiled the king.

" My custom is the law," said Sanders. He dropped his voice till it was so soft as to be little above a whisper.

" Tobolaka," he said, " I hanged your father and, I believe, his father. Now I tell you this—that you shall play this king game just so long as it amuses your people, but you play it without soldiers. And if you gather an army for whatever purpose, I shall come and burn your city and send you the way of your ancestors, for there is but one king in this land, and I am his chief minister."

The face of the king twitched and his eyes fell.

" Lord," he said, using the conventional " Iwa " of his people, " I meant no harm. I desired only to do honour to my wife."

" You shall honour her best," said Sanders, " by honouring me."

" Cicero says——" began Tobolaka in English.

" Damn Cicero ! " snapped Sanders in the same language.

He stayed the day, and Tobolaka did his best to make reparation for his discourtesy. Towards evening Sanders found himself listening to complaints. Tobolaka had his troubles.

" I called a palaver of all chiefs," he explained, " desiring to inaugurate a system analogous to county councils. Therefore I sent to the Akasava, the N'gombi, and the Ochori, their chiefs. Now, sir," said the injured Tobolaka, relapsing into English, " none of these discourteous fellows——"

" Speak in the language of the land, Tobolaka,"
said Sanders wearily.

" Lord, no man came," said the king; " nor
have they sent tribute. And I desired to bring
them to my marriage feast that my wife should
be impressed; and, since I am to be married in
the Christian style, it would be well that these
little chiefs should see with their eyes the practice
of God-men."

" Yet I cannot force these chiefs to your palaver,
Tobolaka," said Sanders.

" Also, lord," continued the chief, " one of
these men is a Mohammedan and an evil talker,
and when I sent to him to do homage to me
he replied with terrible words, such as I would
not say again."

" You must humour your chiefs, king," said
Sanders, and gave the discomfited monarch no
warmer cheer.

Sanders left next day for headquarters, and
in his hurry forgot to inquire further into the
forthcoming wedding feast.

" And the sooner he marries the better," he
said to the Houssa captain. " Nothing tires me
quite so much as a Europeanised-Americanised
native. It is as indecent a spectacle as a niggerised
white man."

" He'll settle down; there's no stake in a country
like a wife," said the Houssa. " I shouldn't wonder
if he doesn't forget old man Cicero. Which chief's
daughter is to be honoured ? "

Sanders shook his head.

"I don't know, and I'm not interested. He might make a good chief—I'm prejudiced against him, I admit. As likely as not he'll chuck his job after a year if they don't 'chop' him—they're uncertain devils, these Akasavas. Civilisation has a big big call for him ; he's always getting letters from England and America."

The Houssa captain bit off the end of a cigar.

"I hope he doesn't try Cicero on Bosambo," he said significantly.

The next day brought the mail—an event.

Usually Sanders was down on the beach to meet the surf-boat that carries the post, but on this occasion he was interviewing two spies who had arrived with urgent news.

Therefore he did not see the passenger whom the *Castle Queen* landed till she stood on the stoep before the open door of the residency.

Sanders, glancing up as a shadow fell across the wooden stoep, rose and temporarily dismissed the two men with a gesture.

Then he walked slowly to meet the girl.

She was small and pretty in a way, rather flushed by the exertion of walking from the beach to the house.

Her features were regular, her mouth was small, her chin a little weak. She seemed ill at ease.

"How do you do?" said Sanders, bewildered by the unexpectedness of the vision. He drew a chair for her, and she sank into it with a grateful little smile, which she instantly checked, as though she had set herself an unpleasant task and was not to be conciliated or turned aside by any act of courtesy on his part.

" And exactly what brings you to this unlikely place ? " he asked.

" I'm Millie Tavish," she said. " I suppose you've heard about me ? "

She spoke with a curious accent. When she told him her name he recognised it as Scottish, on which American was imposed.

" I haven't heard about you," he said. " I presume you are going up-country to a missionary station. I'm sorry—I do not like lady missionaries in the country."

She laughed a shrill, not unmusical laugh.

" Oh, I guess I'm not a missionary," she said complacently. " I'm the queen."

Sanders looked at her anxiously. To women in his country he had conscientious objections ; mad women he barred.

" I'm the queen," she repeated, evidently pleased with the sensation she had created. " My ! I never thought I should be a queen. My grandfather used to be a gardener of Queen Victoria's before he came to N'York——"

" But—— " said the staggered Commissioner.

" It was like this," she rattled on. " When Toby was in Philadelphia at the theological seminary I was a help at Miss Van Houten's— that's the boarding house—an' Toby paid a lot of attention to me. I thought he was joshin' when he told me he was going to be a king, but he's made good all right. And I've written to him every week, and he's sent me the money to come along——"

"Toby?" said Sanders slowly. "Who is Toby?"

"Mr. Tobolaka—King Tobolaka," she said.

A look of horror, which he did not attempt to disguise, swept over the face of the Commissioner.

"You've come out to marry him—a black man?" he gasped.

The girl flushed a deep red.

"That's my business," she said stiffly. 'I'm not asking advice from you. Say, I've heard about you—your name's mud along this old coast, but I'm not afraid of you. I've got a permit to go up the Isisi, and I'm goin'.''

She was on her feet, her arms akimbo, her eyes blazing with anger, for, womanlike, she felt the man's unspoken antagonism.

"My name may be mud," said Sanders quietly, "and what people say about me doesn't disturb my sleep. What they would say about me if I'd allowed you to go up-country and marry a black man would give me bad nights. Miss Tavish, the mail-boat leaves in an hour for Sierra Leone. There you will find a steamer to take you to England. I will arrange for your passage and see that you are met at Southampton and your passage provided for New York."

"I'll not go," she stormed; "you don't put that kind of bluff on me. I'm an American citizeness and no dud British official is going to boss me—so there!"

Sanders smiled.

He was prepared to precipitate matters now to violate treaties, to create crises, but he was not prepared to permit what he regarded as an outrage.

In turn she bullied and pleaded ; she even wept, and Sanders's hair stood on end from sheer fright.

To make the situation more difficult, a luxurious Isisi canoe with twenty paddlers had arrived to carry her to the city, and the headman in charge had brought a letter from her future lord welcoming her in copper-plate English. This letter Sanders allowed the man to deliver.

In the end, after a hasty arrangement, concluded by letter with the captain of the boat, he escorted Millie Tavish to the beach.

She called down on his head all the unhappiness her vocabulary could verbalise ; she threw with charming impartiality the battle of Bannockburn and Bunker's Hill at his stolid British head. She invoked the shades of Washington and William Wallace.

" You shall hear of this," she said as she stepped into the surf-boat. " I'm going to tell the story to every paper."

" Thank you ! " said Sanders, his helmet in his hand. " I feel I deserve it."

He watched the boat making a slow progress to the ship and returned to his bungalow.

C

CHAPTER IV

THE FALL OF THE EMPEROR

" MY poor soul ! " said the Houssa captain. He looked down into the long-seated chair where Sanders sprawled limply.

" And is the owdacious female gone ? " asked the soldier.

" She's gone " said Sanders.

The Houssa clapped his hands, not in applause, but to summon his orderly.

" Ahmet," he said gravely, speaking in Arabic, " mix for the lord Sandi the juice of lemons with certain cunning ingredients such as you know well ; let it be as cool as the hand of Azrael, as sweet as the waters of Nir, and as refreshing as the kisses of houris—go with God."

" I wish you wouldn't fool," said Sanders, irritated.

" This is a crisis of our affairs," said Hamilton the Houssa. " You need a tonic. As for myself, if this had happened to me, I should have been in bed with a temperature. Was she very angry ? "

Sanders nodded.

" She called me a British loafer and a Jew in the same breath. She flung in my face every British aristocrat who had ever married an American heiress ; she talked like the New York correspondent of an Irish paper for five minutes. She threatened me with the whole diplomatic armoury of America and the entire strength of Scottish opinion ; if she could have made up her mind whether she was Scot or just Philadelphia I could have answered her, but when she goaded me into a retort about American institutions she opened her kailyard batteries and silenced me.

The Houssa walked up and down the long bungalow.

" It was impossible, of course," he said seriously. " absolutely impossible. She'll land at Sierra Leone and interview Tullerton—he's the U.S. Consul. I think she'll be surprised when she hears Tullerton's point of view "

Sanders stayed to tiffin, and the discussion of Millie Tavish continued intermittently throughout the meal.

" If I hadn't given Yoka permission to overhaul the engines of the *Zaire*," said Sanders, " I'd start right away for the Isisi and interview Tobolaka. But by this time he'll have her cylinders open. By the way, I've remembered something," he said, suddenly.

He clapped his hands, and Hamilton's orderly came.

" Ahmet," said Sanders, " go quickly to Sergeant Abiboo and tell him to give food to the Isisi boatmen who came this morning. Also that he shall tell them to stay with us, for I have a ' book ' to write to the king."

" On my life," said Ahmet conventionally, and went out.

" I will say what I have to say by letter," said the Commissioner, when the man had gone at a jog-trot across the compound; " and, since he has a swift canoe, he will receive evidence of my displeasure earlier than it would otherwise reach him."

Ahmet came back in five minutes, and with him Abiboo.

" Lord," said the latter, " I could not do as you wish, for the Isisi have gone."

" Gone ! "

" Lord, that is so, for when the lady came back from the ship she went straight away to the canoe and——"

Sanders was on his feet, his face white.

" When the lady came back from the ship," he repeated slowly, " Did she come back ? "

" Master, an hour since. I did not see her, for she came by the short way from the beach to the river-landing. But many saw her."

Sanders nodded.

" Go to Yoka and let him have steam against my coming."

The sergeant's face was blank.

" Lord, Yoka has done many things," he said, " such as removing the *shh-shh* of the engine "— Sanders groaned—" yet will I go to him and speak with him for steam."

" If he's got the cylinder dismantled," said Sanders in despair, " it will be hours before the *Zaire* is ready, and I haven't a canoe that can overtake them."

A Houssa came to the door.

"A telegram for you," said Hamilton, taking the envelope from the man.

Sanders tore it open and read. It was from London :

"Washington wires : 'We learn American girl gone to Isisi, West Africa, to marry native king. Government request you advise authorities turn her back at all costs; we indemnify you against any act of arrest to prevent her carrying plan into execution.' Use your discretion and act. Have advised all magistrates. Girl's name Tavish.—Colonial Office."

He had finished reading when Abiboo returned.

"'To-morrow, two hours before the sun, there will be steam, master,' so said Yoka."

"It can't be helped," said Sanders ; "we'll have to try another way.

* * * *

By swift canoe the Isisi is three days' journey from headquarters. From the Isisi to Ochori city is one day. Tobolaka had time to make a last effort to secure magnificence for his wedding feast.

He sent for his councillor, Cala, that he might carry to Bosambo fine words and presents.

"If he refuses to come for my honour," said Tobolaka, "you shall say to him that I am a man who does not forgive, and that one day I will come to him with an army and there will be war."

" Lord king," said the old man, " you are like an elephant, and the world shakes under your feet."

" That is so," said the king ; " also I would have you know that this new wife of mine is white and a great person in her own country."

" Have no fear, lord," said Cala sagely ; " I will lie to him."

" If you tell me I lie, I will beat you to death, old monkey," said the wrathful Tobolaka. " This is true that I tell you."

The old man was dazed.

" A white woman," he said, incredulously. " Lord, that is shame."

Tobolaka gasped. For here was a sycophant of sycophants surprised to an expression of opinion opposed to his master's.

" Lord," stammered Cala, throwing a lifetime's discretion to the winds, " Sandi would not have this —nor we, your people. If you be black and she be white, what of the children of your lordship ? By Death ! they would be neither black nor white, but a people apart ! "

Tobolaka's fine philosophy went by the board.

He was speechless with rage. He, a Bachelor of Arts, the favoured of Ministers, the Latinist, the wearer of white man's clothing, to be openly criticised by a barbarian, a savage, a wearer of no clothes, and, moreover, a worshipper of devils.

At a word, Cala was seized and flogged. He was flogged with strips of raw hide, and, being an old man, he died.

Tobolaka, who had never seen a man die of

violence, found an extraordinary pleasure in the sight. There stirred within his heart sharp exultation, fierce joys which he had never experienced before. Dormant weeds of unreasoning hate and cruelty germinated in a second to life. He found himself loosening the collar of his white drill jacket as the bleeding figure pegged to the ground writhed and moaned.

Then, obeying some inner command, he stripped first the coat and then the silk vest beneath from his body. He tugged and tore at them, and threw them, a ragged little bundle, into the hut behind him.

Thus he stood, bareheaded, naked to the waist.

His headmen were eyeing him fearfully. Tobolaka felt his heart leap with the happiness of a new-found power. Never before had they looked at him thus.

He beckoned a man to him.

" Go you," he said haughtily, " to Bosambo of the Ochori and bid him, on his life, come to me. Take him presents, but give them proudly."

" I am your dog," said the man, and knelt at his feet.

Tobolaka kicked him away and went into the hut of his women to flog a girl of the Akasava, who, in the mastery of a moment, had mocked him that morning because of his white man's ways.

Bosambo was delivering judgment when the messenger of the king was announced.

" Lord, there comes an Isisi canoe full of arrogance," said the messenger.

" Bring me the headman," said Bosambo.

They escorted the messenger, and Bosambo saw, by the magnificence of his garb, by the four red feathers which stood out of his hair at varying angles, that the matter was important.

" I come from the king of all this land," said the messenger ; " from Tobolaka, the unquenchable drinker of rivers, the destroyer of the evil and the undutiful."

" Man," said Bosambo, " you tire my ears."

" Thus says my king," the messenger went on : " ' Let Bosambo come to me by sundown that he may do homage to me and to the woman I take to wife, for I am not to be thwarted, nor am I to be mocked. And those who thwart me and mock me I will come up against with fire and spear.' "

Bosambo was amused.

" Look around, Kilimini," he said, " and see my soldiers, and this city of the Ochori, and beyond by those little hills the fields where all things grow well ; especially do you look well at those fields by the little hills."

" Lord, I see these," said the messenger.

" Go back to Tobolaka, the black man, and tell him you saw those fields which are more abundant than any fields in the world—and for a reason."

He smiled at the messenger, who was a little out of his depth.

" This is the reason, Kilimini," said Bosambo. " In those fields we buried many hundreds of the Isisi who came against my city in their folly—this was in the year of the Elephants. Tell your king this : that I have other fields to manure. The palaver is finished."

Then out of the sky in wide circles dropped a bird, all blue and white.

Raising his eyes, Bosambo saw it narrowing the orbit of its flight till it dropped wearily upon a ledge that fronted a roughly-made dovecot behind Bosambo's house.

" Let this man have food," said Bosambo, and hastened to examine the bird.

It was drinking greedily from a little trough of baked clay. Bosambo disturbed his tiny servant only long enough to take from its red legs a paper that was twice the size, but of the same substance, as a cigarette-paper.

He was no great Arabic scholar, but he read this readily, because Sanders wrote beautiful characters.

" To the servant of God, Bosambo.

" Peace be upon your house. Take canoe and go quickly down-river. Here is to be met the canoe of Tobolaka, the king of Isisi, and a white woman travels therein. You shall take the white woman, though she will not go with you ; nevertheless you shall take her, and hold her for me and my king. Let none harm her, on your head. Sanders, of the River and the People, your friend, writes this.

" Obey in the name of God."

Bosambo came back to the king's messenger.

" Tell me, Kilimini," he said, " what palaver is this that the king your master has ? "

" Lord, it is a marrying palaver," said the man " and he sends you presents."

" These I accept," said Bosambo ; " but tell me, who is this woman he marries ? "

The man hesitated.

" Lord," he said reluctantly, " they speak of a white woman whom my lord loved when he was learning white men's ways."

" May he roast in hell ! " said Bosambo, shocked to profanity. " But what manner of dog is your master that he does so shameful a thing ? For between night and day is twilight, and twilight is the light of evil, being neither one thing nor the other ; and between men there is this same. Black is black and white is white, and all that is between is foul and horrible ; for if the moon mated with the sun we should have neither day nor night, but a day that was too dark for work and a night that was too light for sleep."

Here there was a subject which touched the Monrovian deeply, pierced his armour of superficial cynicism, overset his pinnacle of self-interest.

" I tell you, Kilimini," he said, " I know white folk, having once been on ship to go to the edge of the world. Also, I have seen nations where white and black are mingled, and these people are without shame, with no pride, for the half of them that is proud is swallowed by the half of them that is shameful, and there is nothing of them but white man's clothing and black man's thoughts."

" Lord," said Kilimini timidly, " this I know, though I fear to say such things, for my king is lately very terrible. Now we Isisi have great sorrow because he is foolish."

Bosambo turned abruptly.

" Go now, Kilimini," he said. " Later I shall see you."

He waved the messenger out of his thoughts.

Into his hut, through this to his inner hut, he went.

His wife sat on the carpeted floor of Bosambo's harem, her brown baby on her knees.

" Heart of gold," said Bosambo, " I go to a war palaver, obeying Sandi. All gods be with you and my fine son.

" And with you, Bosambo, husband and lord," she said calmly ; " for if this is Sandi's palaver it is good."

He left her, and sent for his fighting headman, the one-eyed Tembidini, strong in loyalty.

" I shall take one war canoe to the lower river," said Bosambo. " See to this : fifty fighting men follow me, and you shall raise the country and bring me an army to the place where the Isisi River turns twice like a dying snake."

" Lord, this is war," said his headman.

" That we shall see," said Bosambo.

" Lord, is it against the Isisi ? "

" Against the king. As to the people, we shall know in good time."

* * * *

Miss Millie Tavish, seated luxuriously upon soft cushions under the thatched roof of a deck-house, dreamt dreams of royalty and of an urbane negro who had raised his hat to her. She watched the sweating paddlers as they dug the water rhythmically singing a little song, and already she tasted the joys of dominion.

She had the haziest notion of the new position she was to occupy. If she had been told that she would share her husband with half-a-dozen other women—and those interchangeable from time to time—she would have been horrified.

Sanders had not explained that arrangement to her, partly because he was a man with a delicate mind, and partly because he thought he had solved the problem without such explanation.

She smiled a triumphant little smile every time she thought of him and her method of outwitting him. It had been easier than she had anticipated.

She had watched the Commissioner out of sight and had ordered the boat to return to shore, for standing an impassive witness to her embarkation had been the headman Tobolaka had sent. Moreover, in the letter of the king had been a few simple words of Isisi and the English equivalent.

She thought of many things—of the busy city she had left, of the dreary boarding-house, of the relations who had opposed her leaving, of the little legacy which had come to her just before she sailed, and which had caused her to hesitate, for with that she could have lived in fair comfort.

But the glamour of a throne—even a Central African throne—was upon her—she—Miss Tavish —Millie Tavish—a hired help——

And here was the actuality. A broad river, tree-fringed banks, high rushes at the water edge, the feather-headed palms of her dreams showing at intervals, and the royal paddlers with their plaintive song.

She came to earth as the paddlers ceased, not together as at a word of command but one by one as they saw the obstruction.

There were two canoes ahead, and the locked shields that were turned to the king's canoe were bright with red n'gola—and red n'gola means war.

The king's headman reached for his spear half-heartedly. The girl's heart beat faster.

" Ho, Soka ! "

Bosambo, standing in the stern of the canoe, spoke :

" Let no man touch his spear, or he dies ! " said Bosambo.

" Lord, this is the king's canoe," spluttered Soka, wiping his streaming brow, " and you do a shameful thing, for there is peace in the land."

" So men say," said Bosambo evasively.

He brought his craft round so that it lay alongside the other.

" Lady," he said in his best coast-English, " you lib for go with me one time ; I be good feller ; I be big chap—no hurt 'um—no fight 'um."

The girl was sick with terror. For all she knew, and for all she could gather, this man was a cruel and wicked monster. She shrank back and screamed.

" I no hurt 'um," said Bosambo. " I be dam good chap ; I be Christian, Marki, Luki, Johni : you savee dem fellers ? I be same like."

She fainted, sinking in a heap to the bottom of the canoe. In an instant Bosambo's arm was around her. He lifted her into his canoe as lightly as though she was a child.

Then from the rushes came a third canoe with a full force of paddlers and, remarkable of a savage man's delicacy, two women of the Ochori.

She was in this canoe when she recovered consciousness, a woman bathing her forehead from the river. Bosambo, from another boat, watched the operation with interest.

" Go now," he said to the chief of the paddlers, " taking this woman to Sandi, and if ill comes to her, behold, I will take your wives and your children and burn them alive—go swiftly."

Swiftly enough they went, for the river was high, and at the river head the floods were out.

" As for you," said Bosambo to the king's headman, " you may carry word to your master, saying thus have I done because it was my pleasure."

" Lord," said the head of the paddlers, " we men have spoken together and fear for our lives ; yet we will go to our king and tell him, and if he illtreats us we will come back to you."

Which arrangement Bosambo confirmed.

King Tobolaka had made preparations worthy of Independence Day to greet his bride. He had improvised flags at the expense of his people's scanty wardrobe. Strings of tattered garments crossed the streets, but beneath those same strings people stood in little groups, their arms folded, their faces lowering, and they said things behind their hands which Tobolaka did not hear.

For he had outraged their most sacred tradition—

outraged it in the face of all protest. A rent garment, fluttering in the wind—that was the sign of death and of graves. Wherever a little graveyard lies, there will be found the poor wisps of cloth flapping sadly to keep away devils.

This Tobolaka did not know or, if he did know, scorned.

On another such occasion he had told his councillors that he had no respect for the " superstitions of the indigenous native," and had quoted a wise saying of Cicero, which was to the effect that precedents and traditions were made only to be broken.

Now he stood, ultra-magnificent, for a *lokali* sounding in the night had brought him news of his bride's progress.

It is true that there was a fly in the ointment of his self-esteem. His invitation, couched in the choicest American, to the missionaries had been rejected. Neither Baptist nor Church of England nor Jesuit would be party to what they, usually divergent in their views, were unanimous in regarding as a crime.

But the fact did not weigh heavily on Tobolaka. He was a resplendent figure in speckless white. Across his dress he wore the broad blue ribbon of an Order to which he was in no sense entitled.

In places of vantage, look-out men had been stationed, and Tobolaka waited with growing impatience for news of the canoe.

He sprang up from his throne as one of the watchers came pelting up the street.

" Lord," said the man, gasping for breath, " two war canoes have passed."

" Fool ! " said Tobolaka. " What do I care for war canoes ? "

" But, lord," persisted the man, " they are of the Ochori and with them goes Bosambo, very terrible in his war dress ; and the Ochori have reddened their shields."

" Which way did he come ? " asked Tobolaka, impressed in spite of himself.

" Lord," said the man, " they came from below to above."

" And what of my canoe ? " asked Tobolaka.

" That we have not seen," replied the man.

" Go and watch."

Tobolaka was not as perturbed as his councillors, for he had never looked upon reddened shields or their consequences. He waited for half an hour, and then the news came that the canoe was rounding the point, but no woman was there.

Half mad with rage and chagrin, Tobolaka struck down the man who brought the intelligence. He was at the beach to meet the crestfallen headman, and heard his story in silence.

" Take this man," said Tobolaka, " and all the men who were with him, and bind them with ropes. By Death ! we will have a feast and a dance and some blood ! "

That night the war drums of the Isisi beat from one end of the land to the other, and canoes filled with armed men shot out of little creeks and paddled to the city.

Tobolaka, naked save for his skin robe and his anklets of feathers, danced the dance of quick killing, and the paddlers of the royal canoe were publicly executed—with elaborate attention to detail.

In the dark hours before the dawn the Isisi went out against the Ochori. At the first flash of daylight they landed, twelve thousand strong, in Ochori territory. Bosambo was strongly placed, and his chosen regiments fell on the Isisi right and crumpled it up. Then he turned sharply and struck into the Isisi main body. It was a desperate venture, but it succeeded. Raging like a veritable devil, Tobolaka sought to rally his personal guard, but the men of the Isisi city who formed it had no heart for the business. They broke back to the river.

Whirling his long-handed axe (he had been a famous club swinger in the Philadelphia seminary), Tobolaka cut a way into the heart of the Ochori vanguard.

" Ho, Bosambo ! " he called, and his voice was thick with hate. " You have stolen my wife ; first I will take your head, then I will kill Sandi, your master."

Bosambo's answer was short, to the point, and in English :

" Dam nigger ! " he said

It needed but this. With a yelp like the howl of a wolf, Tobolaka, B.A., sprang at him, his axe swirling.

But Bosambo moved as only a Krooman can move.

There was the flash of a brown body, the thud of an impact, and Tobolaka was down with a steel grip at his throat and a knee like a battering-ram in his stomach.

*   *   *   *

The *Zaire* came fussing up, her decks black with Houssas, the polished barrels of her guns swung out. Sanders interviewed King Tobolaka the First —and last.

The latter would have carried the affair off with a high hand.

" Fortune of war, Mr. Sanders," he said airily. " I'm afraid you precipitated this conduct by your unwarrantable and provocative conduct. As Cicero says somewhere——"

" Cut it out," said Sanders. " I want you, primarily for the killing of Cala. You have behaved badly."

" I am a king and above criticism," said Tobolaka philosophically.

" I am sending you to the Coast for trial," said Sanders promptly. " Afterwards, if you are lucky, you will probably be sent home—whither Miss Tavish has already gone."

CHAPTER V

THE KILLING OF OLANDI

CHIEF of Sanders's spies in the wild country was Kambara, the N'gombi man, resolute, fearless, and very zealous for his lord. He lived in the deep of the N'gombi forest, in one of those unexpected towns perched upon a little hill with a meandering tributary to the great river, half ringing its base.

His people knew him for a wise and silent chief, who dispensed justice evenhandedly, and wore about his neck the chain and medal of his office (a wonder-working medal with a bearded face in relief and certain devil marks).

He made long journeys, leaving his village without warning and returning without notice. At night he would be sitting before his fire, brooding and voiceless ; in the morning he would be missing. Some of his people said that he was a witch-doctor, practising his magic in hidden places of the forest ; others that he changed himself into a leopard by his magic and went hunting men. Figuratively speaking, the latter was near the truth, for Kambara was a great tracker of criminals, and there was none so wily as could escape his relentless search.

Thus, when Bolobo, the chief, plotted a rising, it was Kambara's word which brought Sanders and his soldiers, to the unbounded dismay of Bolobo, who thought his secret known only to himself and his two brothers.

It was Kambara who accomplished the undoing of Sesikmi, the great king ; it was Kambara who held the vaguely-defined border line of the N'gombi country more effectively than a brigade of infantry against the raider and the Arab trader.

Sanders left him to his devices, sending such rewards as his services merited, and receiving in exchange information of a particularly valuable character.

Kambara was a man of discretion. When Olandi of the Akasava came into the N'gombi forest, Kambara lodged him regally, although Olandi was breaking the law in crossing the border. But Olandi was a powerful chief and, ordinarily, a law-abiding man, and there are crimes which Kambara preferred to shut his eyes upon.

So he entertained Olandi for two days—not knowing that somewhere down the little river, in Olandi's camp, was a stolen woman who moaned and wrung her hands and greatly desired death.

For Olandi's benefit the little village made merry, and Tisini, the wife of Kambara, danced the dance of the two buffaloes—an exhibition which would have been sufficient to close the doors of any London music-hall and send its manager to hard labour.

At the same time that Olandi departed, Kambara

disappeared ; for there were rumours of raiding on the frontier, and he was curious in the interests of government.

Three weeks afterwards a man whose face none saw came swiftly and secretly to the frontiers of the Akasava country, and with him came such of his kindred as were closely enough related to feel the shame which Olandi had put upon them.

For Olandi of the Akasava had carried off the favourite wife of the man, though not against her will.

This Olandi was a fine animal, tall and broad of shoulder, muscled like an ox, arrogant and pitiless. They called him the native name for leopard because he wore robes of that beast's skin, two so cunningly joined that a grinning head lay over each broad shoulder.

He was a hunter and a fighting man. His shield was of wicker, delicately patterned and polished with copal ; his spears were made by the greatest of the N'gombi craftsmen, and were burnished till they shone like silver ; and about his head he wore a ring of silver. A fine man in every way.

Some say that he aspired to the kingship of the Akasava, and that Tombili's death might with justice be laid at his door ; but as to that we have no means of knowing the truth, for Tombili was dead when they found him in the forest.

Men might tolerate his tyrannies, sit meekly under his drastic judgments, might uncomplainingly accept death at his hands ; but no man is so weak that he would take the loss of his favourite wife without fighting, and thus it came about that these men came paddling furiously through the black night.

Save for the " flip-flap " of the paddles, as they struck the water, and the little groan which accompanied each stroke, there was no sound.

They came to the village where Olandi lorded it just as the moon cleared the feathery tops of the N'gombi woods.

Bondondo lay white and silent under the moon, two rows of roofs yellow thatched, and in the centre the big rambling hut of the chief, with its verandah propped with twisted saplings.

The secret man and his brothers made fast their two canoes and leapt lightly to land. They made no sound, and their leader guiding them, they went through the street like ghostly shadows.

Before the chief's hut the embers of a dull fire glowed. He hesitated before the doors. Three huts built to form a triangle composed the chief's habitation. To the right and left was an entrance with a hanging curtain of skins.

Likely as not Olandi slept in the third hut, which opened from either of these.

He hesitated a moment, then he drew aside the curtains of the right-hand door and went in, his brother, his uncle, and his two cousins following.

A sleepy voice asked who was there.

" I come to see the lord Olandi," said the intruder.

He heard a rustle at the farthermost end of the room and the creaking of a skin bed.

" What seek you ? " said a voice, and it was that of a man used to command.

" Is that my lord ? " demanded the visitor.

He had a broad-bladed elephant sword gripped fast, so keen of edge that a man might shave the hair from the back of his hand therewith.

" I am Olandi," said the man in the darkness, and came forward.

There was absolute stillness. They who waited could hear the steady breathing of the sleepers ; they heard, too, a " whish ! " such as a civilised man hears when his womenfolk thrust a hatpin through a soft straw shape.

Another tense silence, then :

" It is as it should be," said the murderer calmly, and softly called a name. Somebody came blundering from the inner room sobbing with chokes and gulps.

" Come," said the man, then : " Is the foreign woman there also ? Let her also go with us."

The girl called another in a low voice, and a woman joined them. Olandi was catholic in his tastes and raided indiscriminately.

The first girl shrank back as her husband laid his hand on her arm.

" Where is my lord ? " she whimpered.

" I am your lord," said the secret man dryly ; " as for the other, he has no need of women, unless there be women in hell, which is very likely."

None attempted to stop the party as it went through the street and back to the canoes, though there were wails and moanings in Olandi's hut and uneasy stirrings in the villages.

Men hailed them sharply as they passed, saying,

" Oilo ? " which means, " Who walks ? "   But they made no reply.

Then with the river and safety before them, there arose the village watchman who challenged the party.

He had heard the faint death-cry from Olandi's hut, and advanced his terrible cutting-spear to emphasise his challenge.

The leader leapt at him, but the watchman parried the blow skilfully and brought the blade of his spear down as a man of olden times might sweep his battle-axe.

The other's sword had been struck from his hold, and he put up his defenceless arm to ward off the blow.

Twice the sharp edge of the spear slashed his hand, for in the uncertain light of the moon the watchman misjudged his distance.

Then, as he recovered for a decisive stroke, one of the kinsmen drove at his throat, and the watchman went down, his limbs jerking feebly.

The injured man stopped long enough roughly to dress his bleeding palm, then led his wife, shivering and talking to herself like a thing demented, to the canoe, the second wife following.

In the early hours before the dawn four swift paddlers brought the news to Sanders, who was sleeping aboard the *Zaire*, made fast to the beach of Akasava city.

Sanders sat on the edge of his tiny bed, dangling his pyjama'd legs over the side, and listened thoroughly—which is a kind of listening which absorbs not only the story, but takes into account the inflexion of the teller's voice, the sympathy—or lack of it—the rage, the despair, or the resignation of the story-teller.

"So I see," said Sanders when the man had finished, for all four were hot with the news and eager to supply the deficiencies of the others, "this Olandi was killed by one whose wife he had stolen, also the watchman was killed, but none other was injured."

"None, lord," said one of the men, "for we were greatly afraid because of the man's brethren. Yet if he had sought to stop him, many others would have been killed."

"'If the sun were to set in the river, the waters would boil fish,'" quoted Sanders. "I will find this man, whoever he be, and he shall answer for his crime."

He reached the scene of the killing and made prompt inquiry. None had seen the face of the secret man save the watchman—and he was dead. As for the women—the villagers flapped their arms hopelessly. Who could say from what nation, from what tribes, Olandi stole his women?

One, so other inmates of Olandi's house said, was undoubtedly Ochori; as to the other, none knew her, and she had not spoken, for, so they said, she loved the dead man and was a willing captive.

This Olandi had hunted far afield, and was a hurricane lover and a tamer of women; how perfect a tamer Sanders discovered, for, as the Isisi saying goes, "The man who can bribe a woman's tongue could teach a snake to grind corn."

In a civilised country he would have found written evidence in the chief's hut, but barbarous man establishes no clues for the prying detective, and he must needs match primitive cunning with such powers of reason and instinct as his civilisation had given to him.

A diligent search of the river revealed nothing. The river had washed away the marks where the canoes had been beached. Sanders saw the bodies of both men who had fallen without being very much the wiser. It was just before he left the village that Abiboo the sergeant made a discovery.

There is a certain tree on the river with leaves which are credited with extraordinary curative powers. A few paces from where the watchman fell such a tree grew.

Abiboo found beneath its low branches a number of leaves that had been newly plucked. Some were stained with blood, and one bore the clear impression of a palm.

Sanders examined it carefully. The lines of the hand were clearly to be seen on the glossy surface of the leaf, and in the centre of the palm was an irregular cut, shaped like a roughly-drawn St. Andrew's Cross.

He carefully put the leaf away in his safe and went on to pursue his inquiries.

Now, of all crimes difficult to detect, none offers such obstacles as the blood feud which is based on a woman palaver.

Men will speak openly of other crimes, tell all there is to be told, be willing—nay, eager—to put their sometime comrade's head in the noose, if the murder be murder according to accepted native standards. But when murder is justice, a man does not speak; for, in the near future, might not he stand in similar case, dependent upon the silence of his friends for very life ?

Sanders searched diligently for the murderers, but none had seen them pass. What direction they took none knew. Indeed, as soon as the motive for the crime became evident, all the people of the river became blind. Then it was that Sanders thought of Kambara and sent for him, but Kambara was on the border, importantly engaged.

Sanders pursued a course to the Ochori country.

" One of these women was of your people," he said to Bosambo the chief. " Now I desire that you shall find her husband."

Bosambo shifted his feet uneasily.

" Lord," he said, " it was no man of my people who did this. As to the woman, many women are stolen from far-away villages, and I know nothing. And in all these women palavers my people are as dumb beasts."

Bosambo had a wife who ruled him absolutely, and when Sanders had departed, he writhed helplessly under her keen tongue.

" Lord and chief," she said, " why did you speak falsely to Sandi, for you know the woman of the Ochori who was stolen was the girl Michimi of Tasali by the river ? And, behold, you yourself were in search of her when the news of Olandi's killing came."

"These things are not for women," said Bosambo :
"therefore, joy of my life, let us talk of other
things."

"Father of my child," persisted the girl, "has
Michimi no lover who did this killing, nor a husband?
Will you summon the headman of Tasali by the
river and question him?"

She was interested—more interested than Bosambo.

"God is all-seeing and beneficent," he said
devoutly. "Leave me now, for I have holy thoughts
and certain magical ideas for finding this killer of
Olandi, though I wish him no harm."

       *   *   *   *

Sanders had a trick of accepting alarming state-
ments with a disconcerting calm.

People who essayed the task of making his flesh
creep had no reward for their labours ; his politely
incredulous "O, ko!" which, uttered in certain
tones, means, "Oh, indeed!" made his informant
curl up inwardly.

Komo, pompous to a degree, anxious to impress
his lord with the fact that he, Komo, was no ordinary
chief, but a watchful, zealous, and conscientious
regent, came fussing down the river in a glad sweat
to speak of happenings on the edge of his territory.

Sanders granted the man an immediate audience,
though he arrived in the dark hours of the night.

If you will visualise the scene, you have Sanders
sitting up in bed in his pyjamas, and two Houssas
splashed with rain—for a thunderstorm was raging
—one of whom holds a lantern, all the light necessary

to reveal a reeking Komo, shiny and wet, who, squatting on the floor, is voluble and ominous.

"As is my practice, lord," said Komo, "I watch men and things for your honour's comfort, being filled with a desire to serve you. And thus it is that I have learnt of certain things, dances and spells of evil, which are practised by the Ochori."

"The Ochori ? "

Sanders was puzzled.

"By the Ochori—the trusted."

There was no mistaking the arch turn to his speech; the two words were charged with gentle irony.

"Is Bosambo dead that these things should be ? " asked Sanders dryly. "Or has he perchance joined with the dancers ? "

"Lord," said Komo impressively, "Bosambo dances with his people. For, being chief, he is the first to stamp his foot and say 'Ho!' He, too, assists at sacrifices and is ripe for abominable treachery."

"Oh, indeed ! " said Sanders, with an inward sigh of relief. "Now I tell you this, Komo ; there was once a great lord who trusted no man, nor did he trust his household, his wives, nor his slaves, and he walked ever with his back to the sun so that his shadow should run before him, for he did not trust his shadow. And one day he came to a river in flood, and behold ! his shadow lay before him. And because he feared to turn his back upon his shadow, he plunged in and was drowned."

"Lord, I have heard the story. He was a king, and a great one," said Komo. Sanders nodded.

" Therefore, Komo, heed this : I trust all men—a little. I trust Bosambo much, for he has been my man in fair weather and foul." He turned to the silent Houssas. " Let this man be lodged according to his dignity and give him a present of cloth. The palaver is finished."

And Sanders, drawing the bedclothes up to his neck, the night being cold, turned over and was asleep before the chief and his escort had cleared the verandah.

" A busybody," was Sanders's verdict on Komo ; yet, since there is no smoke without fire, he deemed it advisable to investigate at first hand.

Two days after the crestfallen chief had started on his way home the *Zaire* passed his canoe in midstream, going the same way, and the sight of her white hull and twin smokestacks brought consolation to Komo.

" My lord has considered my words," said he to his headman ; " for at his village they said that the puc-a-puc did not leave till the new moon came, and here he comes, though the old moon is still sowing his rind."

" Chief," said the headman, " you are great in council, and even Sandi hearkens and obeys. You are wiser than an owl, swift and terrible as a hawk, and your voice is like the winds of a storm."

" You speak truly," said Komo, who had no false sense of modesty. " I am also very cunning, as you shall see."

Sanders was indeed beating up to the Ochori country. He was perturbed, not by reason of

Komo's sinister suggestion, but because his spies had been silent. If there were dances in the Ochori country he should have been told, however innocent those dances were.

Pigeons had gone ahead of him to tell of his journey, and he found the first of his agents awaiting him at the junction of the Ikeli with the Isisi.

" Lord, it is true that the Ochori dance," said the man, " yet, knowing your lordship trusted Bosambo, I did not make report."

" There you did wrong," said Sanders ; " for I tell you that if a hawk kills a parrot, or the crocodiles find new breeding-places, I wish to know what there is to know."

He gleaned more of these mysterious revels which Bosambo held in the forest as he grew nearer to the Ochori country, and was more puzzled than ever.

" Master," said the chief of the N'gombi village, " many folk go to the Ochori dance, for Bosambo the chief has a great magic."

" What manner of magic ? "

" Lord, it is a magic with whiteness," and he exhibited his hand proudly.

Straight across the reddish-brown palm was an irregular streak of white paint.

" This the lord Bosambo did," he said, " and, behold, every day this remains will be fortunate for me."

Sanders regarded the sign with every evidence of strong emotion.

Two months before Sanders had sent many tins of white paint with instructions to the Ochori chief that his men should seek out the boundary posts of his kingdom—and particularly those that impinged upon foreign territories—and restore them to startling freshness.

" Many people of the Isisi, N'gombi, and Akasava go to Bosambo," the little chief continued ; " for, behold, this magic of Bosambo's wipes away all soil. And if a man has been guilty of wickedness he is released of punishment. I," he added proudly, " once killed my wife's father *cala cala*, and frequently I have sorrowed because of this and because my wife often reminds me. Now, lord, I am a clean man, so clean that when the woman spoke to me this morning about my faraway sin, I hit her with my spear, knowing that I am now innocent."

Sanders thought rapidly.

" And what do you pay Bosambo for this ? " he asked.

" Nothing, lord," said the man.

" Nothing ! " repeated Sanders incredulously.

" Lord, Bosambo gives his magic freely, saying he has made a vow to strange gods to do this ; and because it is free, many men go to his dance for purification. The lord Kambara, the Silent One, he himself passed at sunrise to-day."

Sanders smiled to himself. Kambara would have an interest in stray confessions of guilt——

That was it ! The meaning of Bosambo's practice came to him in a flash. The painting of hands— the lure of purification ; Bosambo was waiting for the man with the scarred hand.

Sanders continued his journey, tied up five miles

short of the Ochori city, and went on foot through the forest to the place of meeting.

It was dark by the time he had covered half the journey, but there was no need of compass to guide him, even had the path been more difficult to follow. Ahead was a dull red glow in the sky where Bosambo's fires burnt.

Four fires there were, set at the points of an imaginary square. In the centre a round circle of stones, and in the centre again three spears with red hafts.

Bosambo had evidently witnessed, or been participant in, an initiation ceremony of a Monrovian secret society.

Within the circle moved Bosambo, and without it, two or three deep, the moving figures of those who sought his merciful services.

Slowly he moved. In one hand a bright tin of Government paint, in the other a Government brush.

Sanders, from his place of observation, grinned approvingly at the solemnity in which Bosambo clothed the ceremony.

One by one he daubed the men—a flick of the brush, a muttered incantation, and the magic was performed.

Sanders saw Kambara in the front rank and was puzzled, for the man was in earnest. If he had come to scoff he remained to pray. Big beads of perspiration glistened on his forehead, the outstretched hands were shaking.

Bosambo approached him, lifted his brush, peered

D

down, then with a sweep of his arm he drew the
N'gombi chief to him

"Brother," he said pleasantly, "I have need of
you."

Sanders saw what it meant, and went crashing
through the undergrowth to Bosambo's side, and
the yelling throng that had closed round the
struggling pair drew back.

"Lord, here is your man!" said Bosambo, and
forcibly pulled forward Kambara's palm.

Sanders took his prisoner back to the *Zaire*, and
from thenceforward, so far as the crime was concerned, there was no difficulty, for Kambara told
the truth.

"Lord," he said, "my hand alone is in fault;
for, though my people were with me, none struck
Olandi but I. Now do with me what you will, for
my wife hates me and I am sick for sleep."

"This is a bad palaver," said Sanders gravely,
"for I trusted you."

"Lord, you may trust no man," said Kambara,
"when his woman is the palaver. I shall be glad to
die, for I was her dog. And Olandi came and stayed
one night in my village, and all that I was to her
and all that I have given her was as nothing. And now
she weeps all day for him, as does the Ochori woman
I took with her. And, lord, if women worship only
the dead, make an end, for I am sick of her scorn."

Sanders, with his head sunk, his hands clasped
behind, his eyes examining the floor of his cabin—
they were on board the *Zaire*—whistled a tune, a
trick of his when he was worried.

" Go back to your village," he said. " You shall pay the family of Olandi thirty goats and ten bags of salt for his blood."

* * * *

" Master," said Bosambo. " I have great joy in my heart that you did not hang this man, for it seems that Olandi did not die too soon. As for the Ochori girl," he went on, " I would have killed Olandi on her account—only Kambara was there first. This," he added, " I tell you, lord, for your secret hearing, for I knew this girl."

Sanders looked at Bosambo keenly.

" They tell me that you have but one wife, Bosambo," he said.

" I have one," said Bosambo evasively, " but in my lifetime I have many perils, of which the woman my wife knows nothing, for it is written in the Sura of the Djinn, ' Men know best who know most, but a woman's happiness lies in her delusions.' "

CHAPTER VI

THE PEDOMETER

BOSAMBO, the chief of the Ochori, was wont to style himself in moments of magnificent conceit, King of the Ochori, Lord Chief of the Elebi River, High Herd of Untamable Buffaloes and of all Goats.

There were other titles which I forget, but I merely mention his claims in order that I may remark that he no longer refers to the goats of his land. There is a reason.

Hikilari, the wise old chief of the Akasava, went hunting in strange territories. That was the year when game went unaccountably westward, some say through the spell of M'Shimba M'Shamba ; but, as Sanders knew, because of the floods.

Hikilari went by river for three days and across a swamp, he and his hunters, before they found elephant. Then they had a good kill, and his bearers came rollicking back to Akasava city, laden with good teeth, some weighing as much as twc hundred kilos.

It was good fortune, but he paid for it tremendously, for when he yearned to return he was troubled with extraordinary drowsiness, and had strange pains in his head. For this he employed the native remedy, which was binding a wire tightly round his head. None the less he grew no better, and there came a time when Hikilari, the Wise One, rose in the middle of the night and, going out into the main street of the village, danced and sang foolishly, snapping his fingers.

His sons, with his nephews and his brothers, held a palaver, and the elder of his sons, M'Kovo, an evil man, spoke thuswise :

" It seems that my father is sick with the sickness *mongo*, for he is now foolish, and will soon be dead. Yet I desire that no word of this shall go to Sandi. Let us therefore put my father away safely, saying he has gone a long journey ; and, whilst he is absent, there are many things we may do and many enemies of whom we may rid ourselves. And if Sandi comes with the soldiers and says, ' Why did you these things ? ' we shall say, ' Lord, who is chief here ? A madman. We did as he bid ; let it be on his head.' "

The brother of the sick king thought it would be best to kill him privily, but against this the king's son set his face.

" Whilst he is alive he is chief," he said significantly ; " if he be dead, be sure Sandi will find somebody to punish, and it may well be me."

For three days they kept the king to his hut, whilst witch-doctors smeared him with red clay and ingola and chanted and put wet clay on his eyes. At the end of that time they removed him by night to a hastily thatched hut in the forest, and there he was left to M'Kovo's creatures.

Sanders, who knew many things of which he was supposed to be ignorant, did not know this. He knew that Hikilari was a wise man ; that he had been on a journey ; that there were no reasons why he (Sanders) should not make a tour to investigate affairs in the Akasava.

He was collecting hut tax in the N'gombi country from a simple pastoral people who objected on principle to pay anything, when the news came to him that a party of Akasava folk had crossed the Ochori border, raided a village, and, having killed the men, had expeditiously carried away the women and goats.

Sanders was in the midst of an interminable palaver when the news came, and the N'gombi people who squatted at his feet regarded him with expectant hope, a hope which was expressed by a small chief who at the moment had the ear of the assembly.

" Lord, this is bad news," he said in the friendly manner of his kind, " and we will not trouble your lordship any farther with our grievances, which are very small. So, therefore, if on account of our bad crops you remit a half of our taxation, we will go peaceably to our villages saying good words about your honour's justice."

" You shall pay all your taxation," said Sanders brusquely. " I waste my time talking with you. "

" Remit one-third," murmured the melancholy speaker. " We are poor men, and there has been no fish in the river——"

Sanders rose from his seat of state wearily.

" I will return with the moon," he said, " and if all taxes be not paid, there will be sad hearts in this village and sore backs, believe me. The palaver is finished."

He sent one messenger to the chief of the Akasava, and he himself went by a short cut through the forest to the Ochori city, for at the psychological moment a cylinder head on the *Zaire* had blown out.

He reached the Ochori by way of Elebi River, through Tunberi—which was swamp, owing to unexpected, unseasonable, and most atrocious rains. Three days he waded, from knee-deep to waist-high, till his arms ached maddeningly from holding his rifle above the black ooze and mud.

And he came upon hippo and water-snake, and once the " boy " who walked ahead yelled shrilly and went down, and Sanders himself was nearly knocked off his feet by the quick rush of the crocodile bearing his victim to the near-by river.

At the end of three days Sanders came to the higher land, where a man might sleep elsewhere than in trees, and where, too, it was possible to bathe in spring water, unpack shirts from headborne loads and count noses.

He was now a day's march from the Ochori, but considerably less than a day's march from the Ochori army, for two hours after he had resumed his journey he came upon the chief Bosambo and with him a thousand spears.

And Bosambo was naked, save for his kilt of monkey-tails, and in the crook of the arm which carried his wicker shield, he carried his five fighting spears.

He halted his army at the sight of Sanders, and came out to meet him.

" Bosambo," said Sanders quietly, " you do me honour that you bring the pick of your fighting men to guard me."

" Lord," said Bosambo with commendable frankness, " this is no honour to you, for I go to settle an account with the King of the Akasava."

Sanders stood before him, his head perched on one side like a bird's, and he slapped his leg absentmindedly with his pliant cane.

" Behold," he said, " I am he who settles all accounts as between kings and kings and men and men, and I tell you that you go back to your city and sit in patience whilst I do the work for which my lord the King appointed me."

Bosambo hesitated. He was pardonably annoyed.

" Go back to your city, Bosambo," said Sanders gently.

The chief squared his broad shoulders.

" I am your man," he said, and turned without another word.

Sanders stopped him before he had taken half a dozen paces.

" Give me twenty fighting men," he said, " and two canoes. You shall hold your men in check whilst I go about the King's business."

An hour later he was going down-stream as fast as a five-knot current and his swift paddlers could take him.

He came to the Akasava city at noon of the following day, and found it peaceable enough.

M'Kovo, the king's son, came to the beach to meet him.

"Lord Sandi," he said with an extravagant gesture of surprise, "I see that the summer comes twice in one season, for you——"

Sanders was in no mood for compliments.

"Where is the old chief, your father?" he asked.

"Master," said M'Kovo earnestly, "I will not lie to you. My father has taken his warriors into the forest, and I fear that he will do evil."

And he told a story which was long and circumstantial, of the sudden flaming up of an old man's rages and animosities.

Sanders listened patiently.

An unwavering instinct, which he had developed to a point where it rose superior to reason, told him that the man was lying. Nor was his faith in his own judgment shaken when M'Kovo produced his elder men and witnesses to his sire's sudden fit of depravity.

But Sanders was a cunning man and full of guile.

He dropped his hand of a sudden upon the other's shoulder.

"M'Kovo," he said mildly, "it seems that your chief and father is no longer worthy. Therefore you shall dwell in the chief's hut. Yet first you shall bring me the chief Hikilari, and you shall bring him unhurt and he shall have his eyes. Bring him quickly, M'Kovo."

"Lord," said M'Kovo sullenly, "he will not come, and how may I force him, for he has many warriors with him?"

Sanders thought the matter out.

" Go now," he said after a while, " and speak with him, telling him that I await him."

" Lord, that I will do," said M'Kovo, " but I cannot go till night because I fear your men will follow me, and my father, seeing them, will put me to death."

Sanders nodded.

That night M'Kovo came to him ready for his journey, and Sanders took from his pocket a round silver box.

" This you shall hang about your neck," he said, " that your father may know you come from me."

M'Kovo hung the round box by a piece of string and walked quickly toward the forest.

Two miles on the forest path he met his cousins and brothers, an apprehensive assembly.

" My stomach is sick with fear," said his elder cousin Tangiri ; " for Sandi has an eye that sees through trees."

" You are a fool," snarled M'Kovo ; " for Sandi is a bat who sees nothing. What of Hikilari, my father ? "

His younger brother extended the point of his spear and M'Kovo saw that it was caked brown with blood.

" That was best," he said. " Now we will all go to sleep, and in the morning I will go back to Sandi and tell him a tale."

In the morning his relatives scratched his legs with thorns and threw dust over him, and an hour later, artificially exhausted, he staggered to the hut before which Mr. Commissioner Sanders sat at breakfast.

Sanders glanced keenly at the travel-worn figure.

" My friend," he said softly, " you have come a long way ? "

" Lord," said M'Kovo, weak of voice, " since I left you I have not rested save before my father, who sent me away with evil words concerning your honour."

And the exact and unabridged text of those " evil words " he delivered with relish.

Sanders reached down and took the little silver box that lay upon the heaving chest.

" And this you showed to your father ? " he asked.

" Lord, I showed him this," repeated the man.

" And you travelled through the night—many miles ? "

" Master, I did as I have told," M'Kovo replied.

Sanders touched a spring, and the case of the box flew open. There was revealed a dial like that of a watch save that it contained many little hands.

M'Kovo watched curiously as Sanders examined the instrument.

" Look well at this, M'Kovo," said Sanders dryly ; " for it is a small devil which talks truly—and it tells me that you have travelled no farther than a man may walk in the time that the full moon climbs a tree."

The *Zaire* had arrived during the night, and a Houssa guard stood waiting.

Sanders slipped the pedometer into his pocket, gave a characteristic jerk of his head, and Sergeant Abiboo seized his prisoner.

" Let him sit in irons," said Sanders in Arabic,
" and take six men along the forest road and bring
me any man you may find."

Abiboo returned in an hour with four prisoners,
and they were very voluble—too voluble for the safety
of M'Kovo and his younger brother, for by night
Sanders had discovered a forest grave where Hikilari
the wise chief lay.

It was under a tree with wide-spreading branches,
and was eminently suitable for the sequel to that
tragedy.

     *   *   *   *   *

Bosambo was not to blame for every crime laid
at his door. He had a feud with the Akasava,
not without reason. The death of M'Kovo his enemy
was not sufficient to extinguish the obligation, for
the Akasava had spilt blood, and that rankled for
many months. He was by nature a thief, being a
Krooman from the Liberian coast before he came
to be king over the simple and fearful Ochori.

So when all the trouble between the Akasava
and Ochori seemed at rest, Sanders had occasion to
come to the Ochori country in a hurry—and the
river was low.

There is no chart of the big river worth two cents
in the dry season, because unexpected sand banks
come barking up in the fairway, and there are whole
stretches of river wherein less than a fathom of
water runs. Sometimes the boy sitting on the bow
of the *Zaire*, thrusting a pliant rod into the stream,
would cry through his nose that there were two
fathoms of water when there was but one.

He was, as I have beforetime said, of the Kano folk, and somewhat religious, dreaming of a pilgrimage to Mecca, and a green band round his tarboosh.

" I declare to you the glory of God and a fathom and a little."

Bump !

" Get overboard, you talkative devil ! " said Sanders, who was more annoyed because this was the fourteenth bank he had struck since he left headquarters. So the whole crew jumped waist deep into the water, and singing a little song as they toiled, pushed the boat clear.

Sanders struck his thirty-ninth bank just before he came to the village of Ochori, and he landed in a most unamiable mood.

" Bosambo," he said, " I have two minds about you—the one is to hang you for your many wickednesses, the other is to whip you."

" Master," said Bosambo with grave piety, " all things shall be as ordained."

" Have no fear but that it will be one or the other," warned the Commissioner. " I am no dog that I should run from one end of the state to the other because a thieving black man raids in forbidden territory."

Bosambo, whose guilty conscience suggested many reasons for the unexpected visit of the Commissioner, seemed less genuinely astonished.

" Master, I am no nigger," he said, " being related by birth and previous marriages to several kings, also——"

" You are a liar," said Sanders, fuming, " and

related by birth and marriage to the father of liars ; and I did not come to talk about your uninteresting family, but rather to discuss a matter of night raiding."

"As to night raiding" said Bosambo frankly, "I know nothing about that. I went with my councillors to the Akasava, being anxious to see the new chief and tell him of my love ; also," he said piously, "to say certain Christian prayers by the grave of my enemy, for, as you know, lord, our faith teaches this."

"By night you went," said Sanders, ignoring the challenge of "our faith," "and Akasava city may easily be gained in broad daylight ; also, when the Akasava fell upon you, you had many goats tied up in your canoes.

"They were my goats," said Bosambo with dignity. "These I brought with me as a present to the new chief."

In his exasperation Sanders swore long and fluently.

"Blood has paid for blood," he said wrathfully, "and there shall be no more raidings. More than this, you shall stay in this city and shall not move therefrom till you have my word."

"Lord Sandi," said Bosambo, "I hear to obey."

A light of unholy joy came momentarily into the eyes of the Commissioner, flickered a moment, and was gone, leaving his face impassive.

"You know, Bosambo," he said mildly—for him, "that I have great faith in you ; therefore I leave you a powerful fetish, who shall be as me in my absence."

He took from the pocket of his uniform jacket a

certain round box of silver, very pleasant to the touch, being somewhat like a flattened egg.

Sanders had set his pedometer that morning.

" Take this and wear it for my sake," he said.

Bosambo threaded a chain through its loop of silver and hung it about his neck.

" Lord," he said gratefully, " you have done this thing before the eyes of my people, and now they will believe all I tell them regarding your love for me."

Sanders left the Ochori city next morning.

" Remember," he warned, " you do not go beyond the borders of your city."

" Master," said Bosambo, " I sit fasting and without movement until your lordship returns."

He watched the *Zaire* until she was a white speck on the placid face of the water ; then he went to his hut.

Very carefully he removed the silver case from his neck and laid it in the palm of his hand.

" Now, little devil," he addressed it, " who watches the coming and going of men, I think I will learn all about you. O hanger of M'Kovo ! "

He pressed the knob—he had once possessed a watch, and was wise in the way of stem springs—the case flew open, and showed him the little dials.

He shook the instrument violently, and heard a faint clicking. He saw a large hand move across the second of a circle.

Bearing the pedometer in his hand, he paced the length of the village street, and at every pace the instrument clicked and the hand moved. When he was still it did not move.

" Praise be to all gods ! " said Bosambo. " Now

I know you, O Talker ! For I have seen your wicked
tongue wagging, and I know the manner of your
speech."

He made his way slowly back to his hut.

Before the door his new baby, the light of his
eyes, sprawled upon a skin rug, clutching frantically
at the family goat, a staid veteran, tolerant of the
indignities which a small brown man-child might
put upon him. Bosambo stopped to rub the child's
little brown head and pat the goat's sleek neck.

Then he went into the hut, carefully removed the
tell-tale instrument from the chain at his neck, and
hid it with other household treasures in a hole beneath
his bed.

At sundown his *lokali* brought the fighting men
together.

"We go to the Akasava," he said, addressing
them briefly, " for I know a village that is fat with
corn and the stolen goats of the Ochori. Also the
blood of our brothers calls us, though not so loudly
as the goats."

He marched away, and was gone three days, at
the end of which time he returned *minus* three men
—for the Akasava village had resisted his attentions
strenuously—but bringing with him some notable
loot.

News travels fast on the river, especially bad
news, and this reached Sanders, who, continuing
his quest for hut tax, had reached the Isisi.

On the top of this arrived a messenger from the
Akasava chief, and Sanders went as fast as the
Zaire could carry him to the Ochori city.

Bosambo heard of his coming.

" Bring me, O my life and pride," he said to his wife, " a certain silver box which is under my bed ; it is so large and of such a shape."

" Lord," said his wife, " I know the box well."

He slipped the loop of the string that held it over his head, and in all calmness awaited his master's coming.

Sanders was very angry indeed, so angry that he was almost polite to his erring chief.

" Lord," said Bosambo, when the question was put to him, " I have not left my city by day or by night. As you find me, so have I been—sitting before my hut thinking of holy things and your lordship's goodness."

" Give me that box," said Sanders.

He took it in his hand and snapped it open.

He looked at the dials for a long time ; then he looked at Bosambo, and that worthy man returned his glance without embarrassment.

" Bosambo," said Sanders, " my little devil tells me that you have travelled for many miles——"

" Lord," said the bewildered chief, " if it says that it lies."

" It is true enough for me," said Sanders. " Now I tell you that you have gone too far, and therefore I fine you and your people fifty goats, also I increase your taxation, revoke your hunting privileges in the Isisi forest, and order you to find me fifty work-men every day to labour in the Government service."

" Oh, ko ! " groaned Bosambo, standing on one leg in his anguish. " That is just, but hard for I tell you, Lord Sandi, that I did raid the Akasava, yet how your devil box should know this I cannot tell, for I wrapped it in cloth and hid it under my bed."

"You did not carry it?" asked Sanders incredulously.

"I speak the truth, and my wife shall testify," said Bosambo.

He called her by name, and the graceful Kano girl who domineered him came to the door of his hut.

"Lord, it is true," she said, "for I have seen it, and all the people have seen it, even while my lord Bosambo was absent."

She stooped down and lifted her fat baby from the dust.

"This one also saw it," she said, the light of pride in her eyes, "and to please my Lord Bosambo's son, I hung it round the neck of Neta the goat. Did I wrong?"

"Bright eyes," said Bosambo, "you can do no wrong, yet tell me, did Neta the goat go far from the city?"

The woman nodded.

"Once only," she said. "She was gone for a day and a night, and I feared for your box, for this is the season when goats are very restless."

Bosambo turned to his overlord.

"You have heard, O Sandi," he said. "I am in fault, and will pay the price."

"That you will," said Sanders, "for the other goat has done no wrong."

CHAPTER VII

THE BROTHER OF BOSAMBO

BOSAMBO was a Monrovian. Therefore he was a thief. For just as most Swedes are born fair and with blue eyes, and most Spaniards come into this world with swarthy skins, so all Monrovians come into this life constitutionally dishonest.

In another place I have told the story of the chief's arrival in Sanders's territory, of the audacious methods by which he usurped the throne, of that crazy stool of chieftainship, and I hinted at the sudden and unexpected ends, discreditable to Bosambo, which befell the rightful heirs to the chieftainship.

Bosambo was a good man by many standards—Christian and pagan. He ruled his people wisely, and extracted more revenue in one year than any previous chief had taken from the lazy Ochori in ten years.

Incidentally he made an excellent commission, for it was Bosambo's way to collect one for the Government and two for himself. He had in those far-off days, if I remember rightly, been an unruly subject of the President of Liberia. Before a solemn tribunal he had been convicted of having stolen a buoy-bell which had been placed in the fairway to warn navigators of a wreck, and had converted the same to his own use. He had escaped from captivity and, after months of weary travelling, had arrived in the Ochori country.

Sanders had found him a loyal man, and trusted him in all matters affecting good government. There were others who did not trust Bosambo at all—notably certain chiefs of the Isisi, of the Akasava, and of the N'gombi.

These men had measured their wits with the foreigner, the ruler of the Ochori, and been worsted. And because of certain courageous acts performed in the defence of his country it was well known from one end of the territories to the other that Bosambo was "well loved by Sandi," who rumour said—in no complimentary manner—was related to the chief.

As to how this rumour arose Bosambo knows best. It is an elementary fact that travelling news accumulates material in its transit.

Thus it came about that in Monrovia, and in Liberia itself, the fame of the ex-convict grew apace, and he was exalted to a position which he never pretended to occupy. I believe a Liberian journal, published by a black man, or men, so far forgot the heinous offence of which Bosambo stood convicted as to refer to him as "our worthy fellow-citizen, Mr. Bosambo, High Commissioner for the Ochori."

He was a wealthy prince; he was a king. He

was above Commissioner Sanders in point of importance. He was even credited with exercising an influence over the Home Government which was without parallel in the history of the Coast.

Bosambo had relatives along the Coast, and these discovered themselves in ratio with his greatness. He had a brother named Siskolo, a tall, bony, and important man.

Siskolo was first in importance by reason of the fact that he had served on one of his Majesty's ships as a Krooman, that he had a smattering of English, and that he had, by strict attention to business during the period of his contact with white men, stolen sufficient to set him up in Liberia as a native storekeeper.

He was called Mr. Siskolo, and had ambitions at some future period to become a member of the Legislative Council.

It cannot be said with truth that the possession of a brother such as Bosambo was gave him any cause for pride or exaltation during the time when Bosambo's name in Liberia was synonymous with mud. It is even on record that after having denied the relationship he referred to Bosambo—when the relationship was a certainty beyond dispute—as a " low nigger."

When the Liberian Government, in its munificence, offered an adequate reward for the arrest of this law-breaker, Mr. Siskolo, in the most public-spirited way, through the columns of the Press, offered to add a personal reward of his own.

Then the public attitude of Liberia changed

towards Bosambo, and with this change Siskolo's
views upon his brother also underwent a change.
Then came a time when Bosambo was honoured in
his own land, and men spoke of him proudly, and,
as I have indicated, even the public Press wrote of
him in terms of pride.

Now Mr. Siskolo, as is recounted, gathered around
him all people who were nearly or distantly related
to him, and they ranged from the pure aboriginal
grandfather to the frock-coated son-in-law, who ran
a boot factory in Liberia.

" My friends and my comrades," said Mr. Siskolo
oracularly, " you all know that my dear brother
Bosambo has now a large territory, and is honoured
beyond any other coloured man upon this coast.
Now I have loved Bosambo for many years, and
often in the night I have wrestled in prayer for his
safety. Also, I have spoken well about him to all
the white men I have met, and I have on many
occasions sent him large sums of money by messenger.
If this money has not been received," continued Mr.
Siskolo stoutly, " it is because the messengers were
thieves, or robbers may have set upon them by the
wayside. But all my clerks and the people who
love me know that I sent this money, also I have
sent him letters praising him, and giving him great
riches."

He paused, did Mr. Siskolo, and thrust a bony
hand into the pockets of the dress trousers he had
acquired from the valet of the French Consul.

" I have called you together," he said slowly,
" because I am going to make a journey into the

country, and I am going to speak face to face with my beloved brother. For I hear that he has many treasures in his land, and it is not good that he should be so rich, and we, all of us who are related to him in blood, and have loved him and prayed for him for so many years, should be poor."

None of the relations who squatted or sat about the room denied this. Indeed, there was a murmur of applause, not unmixed, however, with suspicion, which was voiced by one Lakiro, popularly supposed to be learned in the law.

" All this is fine talk, Siskolo," he said ; " yet how shall we know in what proportion our dear relation Bosambo will desire to distribute his wealth amongst those of us who love him ? "

This time the applause was unmistakable.

Mr. Siskolo said haughtily : " After I have received treasure from my dear brother Bosambo— my own brother, related to me in blood, as you will all understand, and no cousin, as you are—after this brother of mine, whom I have loved so dearly and for so long, has given me of his treasure, I will take my half, and the other half I will distribute evenly among you."

Lakiro assumed his most judicial air.

" It seems to me," he said, " that as we are all blood relations, and have brought money for this journey which you make, Siskolo, and you yourself, so far as I know, are not finding so much as a dollar, our dear friend and relative Bosambo would be better pleased if his great gifts were distributed equally, though perhaps "—and he eyed the back-country brethren who had assembled, and who were listening uncomprehendingly to a conversation which was half in English and half in Monrovian—" it would be better to give less to those who have no need of money, or less need than we who have acquired by our high education, expensive and luxurious tastes, such as champagne, wine and other noble foods."

For two days and the greater part of two nights the relations of Bosambo argued over the distribution of the booty which they so confidently anticipated. At the end of a fortnight Siskolo departed from Liberia on a coasting steamer, and in the course of time he arrived at Sanders's headquarters.

Now it may be said that the civilised native—the native of the frock coat and the top hat—was Mr. Commissioner Sanders's pet abomination. He also loathed all native men who spoke English—however badly they spake it—with the sole exception of Bosambo himself, whose stock was exhausted within fifty words. Yet he listened patiently as Siskolo unfolded his plan, and with the development of the scheme something like a holy joy took its place in Sanders's soul.

He even smiled graciously upon this black man.

" Go you, Siskolo," he said gently. " I will send a canoe to carry you to your brother. It is true, as you say, that he is a great chief, though how rich he may be I have no means of knowing. I have not your wonderful eyes."

Siskolo passed over the insult without a word.

" Lord Sandi," he said, dropping into the ver-

nacular, for he received little encouragement to
proceed in the language which was Sanders's own.
" Lord Sandi, I am glad in my heart that I go to
see my brother Bosambo, that I may take him by
the hand. As to his treasure, I do not doubt that
he has more than most men, for Bosambo is a very
cunning man, as I know. I am taking him rich
presents, amongst them a clock, which goes by
machinery, from my own store, which could not
be bought at any Coast port under three dollars,
and also lengths and pieces of cloth."

Mr. Siskolo was up early in a morning of July.
Mr. Siskolo in a tall hat—his frock coat carefully
folded and deposited in the little deckhouse on the
canoe, and even his trousers protected against the
elements by a piece of cardboard box—set out on
the long journey which separated him from his
beloved brother.

In a country where time does not count, and where
imagination plays a very small part, travelling is a
pleasant though lengthy business. It was a month
and three days before Siskolo came to the border
of his brother's territory. He was two miles from
Ochori city when he arrayed himself in the hat, the
frock coat, and the trousers of civilisation that he
might make an entry in a manner befitting one who
was of kin to a great and wealthy prince.

Bosambo received the news of his brother's arrival
with something akin to perturbation.

" If this man is indeed my brother," he said, " I
am a happy man, for he owes me four dollars he
borrowed *cala-cala* and has never repaid."

Yet he was uneasy. Relations have a trick of producing curious disorder in their hosts. This is not peculiar to any race or colour, and it was with a feeling of apprehension that Bosambo in his state dress went solemnly in procession to meet his brother.

In his eagerness Siskolo stepped out of the canoe before it was grounded, and waded ashore to greet his brother.

" You are indeed my brother—my own brother Bosambo," he said, and embraced him tenderly. " This is a glorious day to me."

" To me," said Bosambo, " the sun shines twice as bright and the little birds sing very loudly, and I feel so glad, that I could dance. Now tell me, Siskolo," he went on, striking a more practical note, " why did you come all this way to see me? For I am a poor man, and have nothing to give you."

" Bosambo," said Siskolo reproachfully, " I bring you presents of great value. I do not desire so much as a dollar. All I wish is to see your beautiful face and to hear your wise words which men speak about from one end of the country to the other."

Siskolo took Bosambo's hands again.

There was a brief halt whilst Siskolo removed the soaked trousers—" for," he explained, " these cost me three dollars."

Thus they went into the city of the Ochori— arm in arm, in the white man's fashion—and all the city gazed spellbound at the spectacle of a tall, slim man in a frock coat and top hat with a wisp of white shirt fluttering about his legs walking in an attitude of such affectionate regard with Bosambo their chief.

Bosambo placed at the disposal of his brother his finest hut. For his amusement he brought along girls of six different tribes to dance before this interested member of the Ethiopian Church. Nothing that he could devise, nothing that the unrewarded labours of his people could perform, was left undone to make the stay of his brother a happy and a memorable time.

Yet Siskolo was not happy. Despite the enjoyment he had in all the happy days which Bosambo provided of evidence of his power, of his popularity, there still remained a very important proof which Siskolo required of Bosambo's wealth.

He broached the subject one night at a feast given in his honour by the chief, and furnished, it may be remarked in parenthesis, by those who sat about and watched the disposal of their most precious goods with some resentment.

" Bosambo, my brother," said Siskolo, " though I love you, I envy you. You are a rich man, and I am a very poor man and I know that you have many beautiful treasures hidden away from view."

" Do not envy me, Siskolo," said Bosambo sadly, " for though I am a chief and beloved by Sandi, I have no wealth. Yet you, my brother, and my friend, have more dollars than the grains of the sand. Now you know I love you," Bosambo went on breathlessly, for the protest was breaking from the other's lips, " and I do these things without desire of reward. I should feel great pain in my heart if I thought you should offer me little pieces of silver. Yet, if you do so desire, knowing how humble I am before your face, I would take what you gave me not because I wish for riches at your hands, but because I am a poor man."

Siskolo's face was lengthening.

" Bosambo," he said, and there was less geniality in his tone, " I am also a poor man, having a large family and many relations who are also your relations, and I think it would be a good thing if you would offer me some fine present that I might take back to the Coast, and, calling all the people together, say ' Behold, this was given to me in a far country by Bosambo, my brother, who is a great chief and very rich.' "

Bosambo's face showed no signs of enthusiasm.

" That is true," he said softly, " it would be a beautiful thing to do, and I am sick in my heart that I cannot do this because I am so poor."

This was a type of the conversation which occupied the attention of the two brothers whenever the round of entertainments allowed talking space.

Bosambo was a weary man at the end of ten days, and cast forth hints which any but Bosambo's brother would have taken.

It was :

" Brother," he said, " I had a dream last night that your family were sick and that your business was ruined. Now I think that if you go swiftly to your home——"

Or :

" Brother, I am filled with sorrow, for the season approaches in our land when all strangers suffer from boils."

But Siskolo countered with neatness and resolution, for was he not Bosambo's brother ?

The chief was filled with gloom and foreboding. As the weeks passed and his brother showed no signs of departing, Bosambo took his swiftest canoe and ten paddlers and made his way to the I'kan where Sanders was collecting taxes.

" Master," said Bosambo, squatting on the deck before the weary Commissioner, " I have a tale to tell you."

" Let it be such a tale," said Sanders, " as may be told between the settling of a mosquito and the sting of her."

" Lord, this is a short tale," said Bosambo sadly, " but it is a very bad tale—for me."

And he told the story of the unwelcome brother.

" Lord," he went on, " I have done all that a man can do, for I have given him food that was not quite good ; and one night my young men played a game, pretending, in their love of me, that they were certain fierce men of the Isisi, though your lordship knows that they are not fierce, but——"

" Get on ! Get on !" snarled Sanders, for the day had been hot, and the tax-payers more than a little trying.

" Now I come to you, my master and lord," said Bosambo, " knowing that you are very wise and cunning, and also that you have the powers of gods. Send my brother away from me, for I love him so much that I fear I will do him an injury."

Sanders was a man who counted nothing too small for his consideration—always excepting the quarrels of women. For he had seen the beginnings of wars in pin-point differences, and had watched an expedition of eight thousand men march into the bush to settle a palaver concerning a cooking-pot.

He thought deeply for a while, then:

" Two moons ago," he said, " there came to me a hunting man of the Akasava, who told me that in the forest of the Ochori, on the very border of the Isisi, was a place where five trees grew in the form of a crescent——"

" Praise be to God and to His prophet Mohammed," said the pious Bosambo, and crossed himself with some inconsequence.

" In the form of a crescent," Sanders went on, " and beneath the centre tree, so said this young man of the Akasava, is a great store of dead ivory " (*i.e.*, old ivory which has been buried or stored).

He stopped and Bosambo looked at him.

" Such stories are often told," he said.

" Let it be told again," said Sanders significantly.

Intelligence dawned on Bosambo's eyes.

Two days later he was again in his own city, and at night he called his brother to a secret palaver.

" Brother," he said, " for many days have I

thought about you and how I might serve you best. As you know, I am a poor man."

" ' A king is a poor man and a beggar is poorer,' " quoted Siskolo, insolently incredulous.

Bosambo drew a long breath.

" Now I will tell you something," he said, lowering his voice. " Against my old age and the treachery of a disloyal people I have stored great stores of ivory. I have taken this ivory from my people. I have won it in bloody battles. I have hunted many elephants. Siskolo, my brother," he went on, speaking under stress of emotion, " all this I give you because I love you and my beautiful relations. Go now in peace, but do not return, for when my people learn that you are seeking the treasures of the nation they will not forgive you and, though I am their chief, I cannot hold them."

All through the night they sat, Bosambo mournful but informative, Siskolo a-quiver with excitement.

At dawn the brother left by water for the border-line of the Isisi, where five trees grew in the form of a crescent.

*   *   *   *

" Lord," said Bosambo, a bitter and an injured man, " I have been a Christian, a worshipper of devils, a fetish man, and now I am of the true faith—though as to whether it is true I have reason to doubt." He stood before Sanders at head-quarters.

Away down by the little quay on the river his

sweating paddlers were lying exhausted, for Bosambo had come by the river day and night.

Sanders did not speak. There was a twinkle in his eye, and a smile hovered at the corners of his mouth.

"And it seems to me," said Bosambo tragically, "that none of the gods loves me."

"That is your palaver," said Sanders, "and remember your brother loves you more than ever."

"Master," said Bosambo, throwing out his arms in despair, "did I know that beneath the middle tree of five was buried ten tusks of ivory? Lord, am I mad that I should give this dog such blessed treasure? I thought——"

"I also thought it was an old man's story," said Sanders gently.

"Lord, may I look?"

Sanders nodded, and Bosambo walked to the end of the verandah and looked across the sea.

There was a smudge of smoke on the horizon. It was the smoke of the departing mail-boat which carried Siskolo and his wonderful ivory back to Monrovia.

Bosambo raised a solemn fist and cursed the disappearing vessel.

"O brother!" he wailed. "O devil! O snake! Nigger! Nigger! Dam' nigger!"

Bosambo wept.

CHAPTER VIII

THE CHAIR OF THE N'GOMBI

THE N'gombi people prized a certain chair beyond all other treasures.

For it was made of ivory and native silver, in which the N'gombi are clever workers.

Upon this chair sat kings, great warriors, and chiefs of people ; also favoured guests of the land.

Bosambo of the Ochori went to a friendly palaver with the king of the N'gombi, and sat upon the chair and admired it.

After he had gone away, four men came to the village by night and carried off the treasure, and though the King of N'gombi and his councillors searched the land from one end to the other the chair was never found

It might never have been found but for a Mr. Wooling, a trader and man of parts.

He was known from one end of the coast to the other as a wonderful seller of things, and was by all accounts rich.

One day he decided to conquer new worlds and came into Sanders's territory with complete faith in his mission, a cargo of junk, and an intense curiosity.

Hitherto, his trading had been confined to the most civilized stretches of the country—to places where the educated aboriginal studied the rates of exchange and sold their crops forward.

He had long desired to tread a country where heathenism reigned and where white men were regarded as gods and were allowed to swindle on magnificent scale.

Wooling had many shocks, not the least of which was the discovery that gin, even when it was German gin in square bottles, gaudily labelled and enclosed in straw packets, was not regarded as a marketable commodity by Sanders.

" You can take anything you like," said Sanders, waving his fly-whisk lazily, " but the bar is up against alcohol and firearms, both of which, in the hands of an enthusiastic and experimental people, are peculiarly deadly."

" But, Mr. Sanders ! " protested the woolgatherer, with the confident little smile which represented seventy-five per cent. of his stock-in-trade. " I am not one of these new chums straight out from home ! Damn it ! I know the people, I speak all their lingo, from Coast talk to Swaheli."

" You don't speak gin to them, anyway," said Sanders ; " and the palaver may be regarded as finished."

And all the persuasive eloquence of Mr. Wooling did not shift the adamantine Commissioner ; and the trader left with a polite reference to the weather, and an unspoken condemnation of an officious swine of a British jack-in-office which Sanders would have given money to have heard.

Wooling went up-country and traded to the best of his ability without the alluring stock, which had been the long suit in his campaign, and if the truth be told—and there is no pressing reason why it should not—he did very well till he tied up one morning at Ochori city and interviewed a chief whose name was Bosambo.

Wooling landed at midday, and in an hour he had arrayed his beautiful stores on the beach.

They included Manchester cotton goods from Belgium, genuine Indian junk from Birmingham, salt which contained a sensible proportion of good river sand, and similar attractive bargains.

His visit to the chief was something of an event. He found Bosambo sitting before his tent in a robe of leopard skins.

" Chief," he said in the flowery manner of his kind, " I have come many weary days through the forest and against the current of the river, that I may see the greatness of all kings, and I bring you a present from the King of England, who is my personal friend and is distantly related to me."

And with some ceremony he handed to his host a small ikon representing a yellow St. Sebastian perforated with purple arrows—such as may be purchased from any manufacturer on the Baltic for three cents wholesale.

Bosambo received the gift gravely.

" Lord," he said, " I will put this with other

presents which the King has sent me, some of which are of great value, such as a fine bedstead of gold, a clock of silver, and a crown so full of diamonds that no man has ever counted them."

He said this easily; and the staggered Mr. Wooling caught his breath.

"As to this beautiful present," said Bosambo, handling the ikon carelessly, and apparently repenting of his decision to add it to his collection, "behold, to show how much I love you—as I love all white lords—I give it to you, but since it is a bad palaver that a present should be returned, you shall give me ten silver dollars: in this way none of us shall meet with misfortune."

"Chief," said Mr. Wooling, recovering himself with a great effort, "that is a very beautiful present, and the King will be angry when he hears that you have returned it, for there is a saying, 'Give nothing which has been given,' and that is the picture of a very holy man."

Bosambo looked at the ikon.

"It is a very holy man," he agreed, "for I see that it is a picture of the blessed Judas—therefore you shall have this by my head and by my soul."

In the end Mr. Wooling compromised reluctantly on a five-dollar basis, throwing in the ikon as a sort of ecclesiastical makeweight.

More than this, Bosambo bought exactly ten dollars' worth of merchandise, including a length of chiffon, and paid for them with money. Mr. Wooling went away comforted.

It was many days before he discovered amongst

his cash ten separate and distinct dollar pieces that were unmistakably bad and of the type which unscrupulous Coast houses sell at a dollar a dozen to the traders who deal with the unsophisticated heathen.

Wooling got back to the Coast with a profit which was fairly elusive unless it was possible to include experience on the credit side of the ledger.

Six months later, he made another trip into the interior, carrying a special line of talking-machines, which were chiefly remarkable for the fact that the sample machine which he exhibited was a more effective instrument than the one he sold.

Here again he found himself in Ochori city.

He had, in his big trading canoe, one phonograph and twenty-four things that looked like phonographs, and were in point of fact phonographs with this difference, that they had no workable interiors, and phonographs without mechanism are a drug upon the African market.

Nevertheless, Bosambo purchased one at the ridiculously low price offered, and the chief viewed with a pained and reproachful mien the exhaustive tests which Mr. Wooling applied to the purchase money.

" Lord," said Bosambo, gently " this money is good money, for it was sent to me by my half-brother Sandi."

" Blow your half-brother Sandi," said Wooling, in energetic English, and to his amazement the chief replied in the same language :

" You make um swear—you lib for hell one

time—you say damn words you not fit for make angel."

Wooling, arriving at the next city—which was N'gombi—was certainly no angel, for he had discovered that in some mysterious fashion he had sold Bosambo the genuine phonograph, and had none wherewith to beguile his new client.

He made a forced journey back to Ochori city and discovered Bosambo entertaining a large audience with a throaty presentment of the "Holy City."

As the enraged trader stamped his way through the long, straggling street, there floated to him on the evening breeze the voice of the far-away tenor :

> Jer-u-salem! Jer-u-salem!
> Sing for the night is o'er!

"Chief!" said Mr. Wooling hotly, "this is a bad palaver, for you have taken my best devil box, which I did not sell you."

> Last night I lay a sleeping,
> There came a dream so fair.

sang the phonograph soulfully.

"Lord," said Bosambo, "this devil box I bought —paying you with dollars which your lordship ate fearing they were evil dollars."

"By your head, you thief!" swore Wooling. "I sold you this." And he produced from under his arm the excellent substitute.

"Lord," said Bosambo, humbly enough, "I am sorry."

He switched off the phonograph. He dismounted the tin horn with reluctant fingers; with his own hands he wrapped it in a piece of the native matting and handed it to the trader, and Wooling, who had expected trouble, "dashed" his courteous host a whole dollar.

"Thus I reward those who are honest," he said magnificently.

"Master," said Bosambo, "that we may remember one another kindly, you shall keep one half of this and I the other"

And with no effort he broke the coin in half, for it was made of metal considerably inferior to silver.

Wooling was a man not easily abashed, yet it is on record that in his agitation he handed over a genuine dollar and was half way back to Akasava city before he realised his folly. Then he laughed to himself, for the phonograph was worth all the trouble, and the money.

That night he assembled the Akasava to hear the "Holy City"—only to discover that he had again brought away from Ochori city the unsatisfactory instrument he had taken.

In the city of the Ochori all the night a wheezy voice acclaimed Jerusalem to the admiration and awe of the Ochori people.

"It is partly your own fault," said Sanders, when the trader complained. "Bosambo was educated in a civilised community, and naturally has a way with his fingers which less gifted people do not possess."

" Mr. Sanders," said the woolgatherer earnestly, " I've traded this coast, man and boy, for sixteen years, and there never was and there never will be," he spoke with painful emphasis, " an eternally condemned native nigger in this inevitably-doomed-by-Providence world who can get the better of Bill Wooling."

All this he said, employing in his pardonable exasperation, certain lurid similes which need not be reproduced.

" I don't like your language," said Sanders, " but I admire your determination."

Such was the determination of Mr. Wooling, in fact, that a month later he returned with a third cargo, this time a particularly fascinating one, for it consisted in the main of golden chains of surprising thickness which were studded at intervals with very rare and precious pieces of coloured glass.

" And this time," he said to the unmoved Commissioner, who for want of something better to do, had come down to the landing-stage to see the trader depart, " this time this Bosambo is going to get it abaft the collar."

" Keep away from the N'gombi people," said Sanders, " they are fidgety—that territory is barred to you."

Mr. Wooling made a resentful noise, for he had laid down an itinerary through the N'gombi country, which is very rich in gum and rubber.

He made a pleasant way through the territories, for he was a glib man and had a ready explanation for those who complained bitterly about the failing properties of their previous purchases.

He went straight to the Ochori district. There lay the challenge to his astuteness and especial gifts. He so far forgot the decencies of his calling as to come straight to the point.

" Bosambo," he said, " I have brought you very rare and wonderful things. Now I swear to you by," he produced a bunch of variegated deities and holy things with characteristic glibness, " that these chains," he spread one of particular beauty for the other's admiration, " are more to me than my very life. Yet for one tusk of ivory this chain shall be yours."

" Lord," said Bosambo, handling the jewel reverently, " what virtue has this chain ? "

" It is a great killer of enemies," said Wooling enthusiastically ; " it protects from danger and gives courage to the wearer ; it is worth two teeth, but because I love you and because Sandi loves you I will give you this for one."

Bosambo pondered.

" I cannot give you teeth," he said, " yet I will give you a stool of ivory which is very wonderful."

And he produced the marvel from a secret place in his hut.

It was indeed a lovely thing and worth many chains.

" This," said Bosambo, with much friendliness,

" you will sell to the N'gombi, who are lovers of such things, and they will pay you well."

Wooling came to the N'gombi territory with the happy sense of having purchased fifty pounds for fourpence, and entered it, for he regarded official warnings as the expression of a poor form of humour.

He found the N'gombi (as he expected) in a mild and benevolent mood. They purchased by public subscription one of his beautiful chains to adorn the neck of their chief, and they fêted him, and brought dancing women from the villages about, to do him honour.

They expressed their love and admiration for Sandi volubly, until, discovering that their enthusiasm awoke no responsive thrill in the heart or the voice of their hearer, they tactfully volunteered the opinion that Sandi was a cruel and oppressive master.

Whereupon Wooling cursed them fluently, calling them eaters of fish and friends of dogs; for it is against the severe and inborn creed of the Coast to allow a nigger to speak disrespectfully of a white man—even though he is a Government officer.

" Now listen all people," said Wooling; " I have a great and beautiful object to sell you——"

*   *   *   *

Over the tree-tops there rolled a thick yellow cloud which twisted and twirled into fantastic shapes.

Sanders walked to the bow of the *Zaire* to examine the steel hawser. His light-hearted crew had a trick of "tying-up" to the first dead and rotten stump which presented itself to their eyes.

For once they had found a firm anchorage. The hawser was clamped about the trunk of a strong young copal which grew near the water's edge. An inspection of the stern hawser was as satisfactory.

"Let her rip," said Sanders, and the elements answered *instanter*.

A jagged blue streak of flame leapt from the yellow skies, a deafening crack-crash of thunder broke overhead, and suddenly a great wind smote the little steamer at her shelter, and set the tops of the trees bowing with grave unanimity.

Sanders reached his cabin, slid back the door, and pulled it back to its place after him.

In the stuffy calm of his cabin he surveyed the storm through his window, for his cabin was on the top deck and he could command as extensive a view of the scene as it was possible to see from the little bay.

He saw the placid waters of the big river lashed to waves; saw tree after tree sway and snap as M'shimba M'shamba stalked terribly through the forest; heard the high piercing howl of the tempest punctuated by the ripping crack of the thunder, and was glad in the manner of the Philistine that he was not where other men were.

Night came with alarming swiftness.

Half an hour before, at the first sign of the cyclone, he had steered for the first likely mooring. In the last rays of a blood-red sun he had brought his boat to land.

Now it was pitch dark—almost as he stood watching the mad passion of the storm it faded first into grey, then into inky blue—then night obliterated the view.

He groped for the switch and turned it, and the cabin was filled with soft light. There was a small telephone connecting the cabin with the Houssa guard, and he pressed the button and called the attention of Sergeant Abiboo to his need.

" Get men to watch the hawsers," he instructed, and a guttural response answered him.

Sanders was on the upper reaches of the Tesai, in *terra incognita*. The tribes around were frankly hostile, but they would not venture about on a night like this.

Outside, the thunder cracked and rolled and the lightning flashed incessantly.

Sanders found a cheroot in a drawer and lighted it, and soon the cabin was blue with smoke, for it had been necessary to close the ventilator. Dinner was impossible under the conditions. The galley fire would be out. The rain which was now beating fiercely on the cabin windows would have long since extinguished the range.

Sanders walked to the window and peered out. He switched off the light, the better to observe the condition outside. The wind still howled, the lightning flickered over the tree-tops, and above the sound of wind and rushing water came the sulky grumble of thunder.

But the clouds had broken, and fitful beams of moonlight showed on the white-crested waves.

Suddenly Sanders stepped to the door and slid it open.

He sprang out upon the deck.

The waning forces of the hurricane caught him and flung him back against the cabin, but he grasped a convenient rail and pulled himself to the side of the boat.

Out in mid-stream he had seen a canoe and had caught a glimpse of a white face.

"Noka! Abiboo!" he roared. But the wind drowned his voice. His hand went to his hip— a revolver cracked, men came along the deck, hand over hand, grasping the rails.

In dumb show he indicated the boat.

A line was flung, and out of the swift control current of the stream they drew all that was left of Mr. Wooling.

He gained enough breath to whisper a word— it was a word that set the *Zaire* humming with life. There was steam in the boiler—Sanders would not draw fires in a storm which might snap the moorings and leave the boat at the mercy of the elements.

" . . . they chased me down river . . . I shot a few . . . but they came on . . . then the storm struck us . . . they're not far away."

Wrapped in a big overcoat and shivering in spite of the closeness of the night, he sat by Sanders, as he steered away into the seething waters of the river.

"What's the trouble?"

The wind blew his words to shreds, but the

huddled figure crouching at his side heard him and answered.

" What's that ? " asked Sanders, bending his head.

Wooling shouted again.

Sanders shook his head.

The two words he caught were " chair " and " Bosambo."

They explained nothing to Sanders at the moment.

CHAPTER IX

THE KI-CHU

THE messenger from Sakola, the chief of the little folk who live in the bush, stood up. He was an ugly little man, four feet in height and burly, and he wore little save a small kilt of grass.

Sanders eyed him thoughtfully, for the Commissioner knew the bush people very well.

"You will tell your master that I, who govern this land for the King, have sent him lord's pleasure in such shape as rice and salt and cloth, and that he has sworn by death to keep the peace of the forest. Now I will give him no further present——"

"Lord," interrupted the little bushman outrageously, "he asks of your lordship only this cloth to make him a fine robe, also ten thousand beads for his wives, and he will be your man for ever."

Sanders showed his teeth in a smile in which could be discovered no amusement.

"He shall be my man," he said significantly

The little bushman shuffled his uneasy feet.

"Lord, it will be death to me to carry your proud message to our city, for we ourselves are very proud people, and Sakola is a man of greater pride than any."

" The palaver is finished," said Sanders, and the little man descended the wooden steps to the sandy garden path.

He turned, shading his eyes from the strong sun in the way that bushmen have, for these folk live in the solemn half-lights of the woods and do not love the brazen glow of the heavens.

" Lord," he said timidly, " Sakola is a terrible man, and I fear that he will carry his spears to a killing."

Sanders sighed wearily and thrust his hands into the deep pockets of his white jacket.

" Also I will carry my spears to a killing," he said. " O ko! Am I a man of the Ochori that I should fear the chattering of a bushman ? "

Still the man hesitated.

He stood balancing a light spear on the palm of his hand, as a man occupied with his thoughts will play with that which is in reach. First he set it twirling, then he spun it deftly with his finger and thumb.

" I am the servant of Sakola," he said simply.

Like a flash of light his thin brown arm swung out, the spear held stiffly.

Sanders fired three times with his automatic Colt, and the messenger of the proud chief Sakola went down sideways like a drunken man.

Sergeant Abiboo, revolver in hand, leapt through a window of the bungalow to find his master moving a smouldering uniform jacket—you cannot fire

through your pocket with impunity—and eyeing
the huddled form of the fallen bushman with a
thoughtful frown.

" Carry him to the hospital," said Sanders.
" I do not think he is dead."

He picked up the spear and examined the point.

There was lock-jaw in the slightest scratch of
it, for these men are skilled in the use of tetanus.

The compound was aroused. Men had come
racing over from the Houssa lines, and a rough
stretcher was formed to carry away the débris.

Thus occupied with his affairs Sanders had no
time to observe the arrival of the mail-boat, and
the landing of Mr. Hold.

The big American filled the only comfortable
seat in the surf-boat, but called upon his familiar
gods to witness the perilous character of his sitting.

He was dressed in white, white irregularly splashed
with dull grey patches of sea-water, for the Kroomen
who manipulated the sweeps had not the finesse,
nor the feather stroke, of a Harvard eight, and
they worked independently.

He was tall and broad and thick—the other way.
His face was clean-shaven, and he wore a cigar
two points south-west.

Yet, withal, he was a genial man, or the lines
about his face lied cruelly.

Nearing the long yellow beach where the waters
were engaged everlastingly in a futile attempt to
create a permanent sea-wall, his references to home
ceased, and he confined himself to apprehensive
" huh's ! "

"Huh!" he grunted, as the boat was kicked into the air on the heels of a playful roller. "Huh!" he said, as the big surfer dropped from the ninth floor to a watery basement. "Huh—oh!" he exclaimed—but there was no accident; the boat was gripped by wading landsmen and slid to safety.

Big Ben Hold rolled ashore and stood on the firm beach looking resentfully across the two miles of water which separated him from the ship.

"Orter build a dock," he grumbled.

He watched, with a jealous eye, the unloading of his kit, checking the packing cases with a piece of green chalk he dug up from his waistcoat pocket and found at least one package missing. The only important one, too. Is this it? No! Is that it? No! Is that—ah, yes, that was it.

He was sitting on it.

"Suh," said a polite Krooman, "you lib for dem k'miss'ner?"

"Hey?"

"Dem Sandi—you find um?"

"Say," said Mr. Hold, "I don't quite get you—I want the Commissioner—the Englishman—savee."

Later, he crossed the neat and spotless compound of the big, cool bungalow, where, on the shaded verandah, Mr. Commissioner Sanders watched the progress of the newcomer without enthusiasm.

For Sanders had a horror of white strangers; they upset things; had fads; desired escorts for passing through territories where the natural desire for war and an unnatural fear of Government reprisal were always delicately balanced.

"Glad to see you. Boy, push that chair along; sit down, won't you?"

Mr. Hold seated himself gingerly.

"When a man turns the scale at two hundred and thirty-eight pounds," grumbled Big Ben pleasantly, "he sits mit circumspection, as a Dutch friend of mine says." He breathed a long, deep sigh of relief as he settled himself in the chair and discovered that it accepted the strain without so much as a creak.

Sanders waited with an amused glint in his eyes.

"You'd like a drink?"

Mr. Hold held up a solemn hand. "Tempt me not," he adjured. "I'm on a diet—I don't look like a food crank, do I?"

He searched the inside pocket of his coat with some labour. Sanders had an insane desire to assist him. It seemed that the tailor had taken a grossly unfair advantage of Mr. Hold in building the pocket so far outside the radius of his short arm.

"Here it is!"

Big Ben handed a letter to the Commissioner, and Sanders opened it. He read the letter very carefully, then handed it back to its owner. And as he did so he smiled with a rare smile, for Sanders was not easily amused.

"You expect to find the ki-chu here?" he asked.

Mr. Hold nodded.

"I have never seen it," said Sanders; "I have heard of it; I have read about it, and I have listened to people who have passed through my territories and who have told me that they have seen it with, I am afraid, disrespect."

Big Ben leant forward, and laid his large and earnest hand on the other's knee.

"Say, Mr. Sanders," he said, "you've probably heard of me—I'm Big Ben Hold—everybody knows me, from the Pacific to the Atlantic. I am the biggest thing in circuses and wild beast expositions the world has ever seen. Mr. Sanders, I have made money, and I am out of the show business for a million years, but I want to see that monkey ki-chu——"

" But——"

" Hold hard." Big Ben's hand arrested the other. "Mr. Sanders, I have made money out of the ki-chu. Barnum made it out of the mermaid, but my fake has been the tailless ki-chu, the monkey that is so like a man that no alderman dare go near the cage for fear people think the ki-chu has escaped. I've run the ki-chu from Seattle to Portland, from Buffalo to Arizona City. I've had a company of militia to regulate the crowds to see the ki-chu. I have had a whole police squad to protect me from the in-fu-ri-ated populace when the ki-chu hasn't been up to sample. I have had ki-chus of every make and build. There are old ki-chus of mine that are now raising families an' mortgages in the Middlewest; there are ki-chus who are running East-side saloons with profit to themselves and their dude sons, there——"

" Yes, yes !" Sanders smiled again. " But why ?"

" Let me tell you, sir," again Big Ben held up his beringed hand, " I am out of the business—good ! But, Mr. Sanders, sir, I have a conscience." He laid his big hand over his heart and lowered his voice. " Lately I have been worrying over this old ki-chu. I have built myself a magnificent dwelling in Boston ; I have surrounded myself with the evidences and services of luxury ; but there is a still small voice which penetrates the sound-proof walls of my bedroom, that intrudes upon the silences of my Turkish bath—and the voice says, ' Big Ben Hold—there aren't any ki-chu ; you're a fake ; you're a swindler ; you're a green goods man ; you're rollin' in riches secured by fraud.' Mr. Sanders, I must see a ki-chu ; I must have a real ki-chu if I spend the whole of my fortune in getting it " ; he dropped his voice again, " if I lose my life in the attempt."

He stared with gloom, but earnestness, at Sanders, and the Commissioner looked at him thoughtfully. And from Mr. Hold his eyes wandered to the gravelled path outside, and the big American, following his eyes, saw a discoloured patch.

" Somebody been spillin' paint ? " he suggested. " I had——"

Sanders shook his head.

" That's blood," he said simply, and Mr. Hold jerked.

" I've just shot a native," said Sanders, in a conversational tone. " He was rather keen on spearing me, and I was rather keen on not being speared. So I shot him."

" Dead ? "

" Not very ! " replied the Commissioner. " As
a matter of fact I think I just missed putting him
out—there's an Eurasian doctor looking him over
just now, and if you're interested, I'll let you
know how he gets along."

The showman drew a long breath.

" This is a nice country," he said.

Sanders nodded. He called his servants and
gave directions for the visitor's comfortable housing.

A week later, Mr. Hold embarked for the upper
river with considerable misgiving, for the canoe
which Sanders had placed at his disposal seemed,
to say the least, inadequate.

It was at this time that the Ochori were in some
disfavour with the neighbouring tribes, and a
small epidemic of rebellion and warfare had sustained the interest of the Commissioner in his
wayward peoples.

First, the N'gombi people fought the Ochori,
then the Isisi folk went to war with the Akasava
over a question of women, and the Ochori went
to war with the Isisi, and between whiles, the
little bush folk warred indiscriminately with everybody, relying on the fact that they lived in the
forest and used poisoned arrows.

They were a shy, yet haughty people, and they
poisoned their arrows with tetanus, so that all
who were wounded by them died of lock-jaw after
many miserable hours.

They were engaged in harrying the Ochori people,
when Mr. Commissioner Sanders, who was not

unnaturally annoyed, came upon the scene with fifty Houssas and a Maxim gun, and although the little people were quick, they did not travel as fast as a well-sprayed congregation of .303 bullets, and they sustained a few losses.

Then Timbani, the little chief of the Lesser Isisi, spoke to his people assembled :

" Let us fight the Ochori, for they are insolent, and their chief is a foreigner and of no consequence."

And the fighting men of the tribe raised their hands and cried, " Wa ! "

Timbani led a thousand spears into the Ochori country, and wished he had chosen another method of spending a sultry morning, for whilst he was burning the village of Kisi, Sanders came with vicious unexpectedness upon his flank, from the bush country.

Two companies of Houssas shot with considerable accuracy at two hundred yards, and when the spears were stacked and the prisoners squatted, resigned but curious, in a circle of armed guards, Timbani realised that it was a black day in his history.

" I only saw this, lord," he said, " that Bosambo has made me a sorrowful man, for if it were not for his prosperity, I should never have led my men against him, and I should not be here before your lordship, wondering which of my wives would mourn me most."

" As to that, Timbani," said Sanders, " I have no means of knowing. Later, when you work in the Village of Irons, men will come and tell you."

Timbani drew a deep breath. " Then my lord does not hang me ? " he asked.

" I do not hang you because you are a fool," said Sanders. " I hang wicked men, but fools I send to hard labour."

The chief pondered. " It is in my mind, Lord Sandi," he said, " that I would as soon hang for villainy as live for folly."

" Hang him ! " said Sanders, who was in an obliging mood.

But when the rope was deftly thrown across the limb of a tree, Timbani altered his point of view, electing to drag out an ignominious existence. Wherein he was wise, for whilst there is life there is scope, if you will pardon the perversion.

To the Village of Irons went Timbani, titular chief of the Lesser Isisi, and found agreeable company there, and, moreover, many predecessors, for the Isisi folk are notoriously improvident in the matter of chiefs.

They formed a little community of their own, they and their wives, and at evening time they would sit round a smouldering log of gum wood, their red blankets about their shoulders, and tell stories of their former grandeur, and as they moved the loose shackles about their feet would jingle musically.

On a night when the Houssa sentries, walking along raised platforms, which commanded all views of the prisoners' compound, were unusually lax, Timbani effected his escape, and made the best of his way across country to the bush lands. The

Journey occupied two months in time, but native folk are patient workers, and there came a spring morning, when Timbani, lean and muscular, stood in the presence of Sakola, the bush king.

" Lord," said he, though he despised all bushmen, " I have journeyed many days to see you, knowing that you are the greatest of all kings."

Sakola sat on a stool carved crudely to represent snakes. He was under four feet in height, and was ill-favoured by bush standards—and the bush standard is very charitable. His big head, his little eyes, the tuft of wiry whisker under his chin, the high cheek bones, all contributed to the unhappy total of ugliness.

He was fat in an obvious way, and had a trick of scratching the calf of his leg as he spoke.

He blinked up at the intruder—for intruder he was, and the guard at each elbow was eloquent of the fact.

" Why do you come here ? " croaked Sakola.

He said it in two short words, which literally mean, " Here—why ? "

" Master of the forest," explained Timbani glibly, " I come because I desire your happiness. The Ochori are very rich, for Sandi loves them. If you go to them Sandi will be sorry."

The bushman sniffed. " I went to them and I was sorry," he said, significantly.

" I have a ju-ju," said the eager Timbani, alarmed at the lack of enthusiasm. " He will help you ; and will give you signs."

Sakola eyed him with a cold and calculating eye.

In the silence of the forest they stared at one another, the escaped prisoner with his breast filled with hatred of his overlord, and the squat figure on the stool.

Then Sakola spoke.

"I believe in devils," he said, "and I will try your ju-ju. For I will cut you a little and tie you to the top of my tree of sacrifice. And if you are alive when the sun sets, behold I will think that is a good sign, and go once again into the Ochori land. But if you are dead, that shall be a bad sign, and I will not fight."

When the sun set behind the golden green of the tree tops, the stolid crowd of bushmen who stood with their necks craning and their faces upturned, saw the poor wreck of a man twist slowly.

"That is a good sign," said Sakola, and sent messengers through the forest to assemble his fighting men.

Twice he flung a cloud of warriors into the Ochori territory. Twice the chiefs of the Ochori hurled back the invader, slaying many and taking prisoners.

About these prisoners. Sanders, who knew something of the gentle Ochori, had sent definite instructions.

When news of the third raid came, Bosambo gave certain orders.

"You march with food for five days," he said to the heads of his army, "and behold you shall feed all the prisoners you take from the grain you carry, giving two hands to each prisoner and one to yourself."

" But, lord," protested the chief, " this is mad-
ness, for if we take many prisoners we shall starve."

Bosambo waved him away. " M'bilini," he said,
with dignity, " once I was a Christian—just as my
brother Sandi, was once a Christian—and we
Christians are kind to prisoners."

" But, lord Bosambo," persisted the other, " if
we kill our prisoners and do not bring them back it
will be better for us."

" These things are with the gods," said the pious
Bosambo vaguely.

So M'bilini went out against the bushmen and
defeated them. He brought back an army well fed,
but without prisoners.

Thus matters stood when Big Ben Hold came
leisurely up the river, his canoe paddled close in
shore, for here the stream does not run so swiftly.

It had been a long journey, and the big man in
the soiled white ducks showed relief as he stepped
ashore on the Ochori beach and stretched his legs.

He had no need to inquire which of the party
approaching him was Bosambo. For the chief wore
his red plush robe, his opera hat, his glass bracelets,
and all the other appurtenances of his office.

Big Ben had come up the river in his own good
time and was now used to the way of the little
chiefs.

His interpreter began a conversational oration,
but Bosambo cut him short.

" Nigger," he said, in English, " you no speak 'um
—I speak 'um fine English. I know Luki, Marki,
John, Judas—all fine fellers. You, sah," he addressed

the impressed Mr. Hold, " you lib for me ? Sixpence —four dollar, good-night, I love you, mister ! "

He delivered his stock breathlessly.

" Fine ! " said Mr. Hold, awestricken and dazed.

He felt at home in the procession which marched in stately manner towards the chief's hut ; it was as near a circus parade as made no difference.

Over a dinner of fish he outlined the object of his search and the reason for his presence.

It was a laborious business, necessitating the employment of the despised and frightened interpreter until the words " ki-chu " were mentioned, whereupon Bosambo brightened up.

" Sah," interrupted Bosambo, " I savee al dem talk ; I make 'um English one time good."

" Fine," said Mr. Hold gratefully, " I get you, Steve."

" You lookum ki-chu," continued Bosambo, " you no find 'um ; I see 'um ; I am God-man—Christian ; I savee Johnny Baptist ; Peter cut 'um head off— dam' bad man ; I savee Hell an' all dem fine fellers."

" Tell him——" began Big Ben.

" I spik English same like white man ! " said the indignant Bosambo. " You no lib for make dem feller talky talk—I savee dem ki-chu."

Big Ben sighed helplessly. All along the river the legend of the ki-chu was common property. Everybody knew of the ki-chu—some had seen those who had seen it. He was not elated that Bosambo should be counted amongst the faithful.

For the retired showman had by this time almost

salved his conscience. It was enough, perhaps, that evidence of the ki-chu's being should be afforded— still he would dearly have loved to carry one of the alleged fabulous creatures back to America with him.

He had visions of a tame ki-chu chained to a stake on his Boston lawn ; of a ki-chu sitting behind gilded bars in a private menagerie annexe.

" I suppose," said Mr. Hold, " you haven't seen a ki-chu—you savee—you no look 'um ? "

Bosambo was on the point of protesting that the ki-chu was a familiar object of the landscape when a thought occurred to him.

" S'pose I find 'um ki-chu you dash* me plenty dollar ? " he asked.

" If you find me that ki-chu," said Mr. Hold slowly, and with immense gravity, " I will pay you a thousand dollars."

Bosambo rose to his feet, frankly agitated.

" Thousan' dollar ? " he repeated.

" A thousand dollars," said Big Ben with the comfortable air of one to whom a thousand dollars was a piece of bad luck.

Bosambo put out his hand and steadied himself against the straw-plaited wall of his hut.

" You make 'um hundred dollar ten time ? " he asked, huskily, " you make 'um book ? "

" I make 'um book," said Ben, and in a moment of inspiration drew a note-book from his pocket and carefully wrote down the substance of his offer.

He handed the note to the chief, and Bosambo stared at it uncomprehendingly.

* Give.

" And," said Big Ben, confidentially leaning across and tapping the knee of the standing chief with the golden head of his cane, " if you——"

Bosambo raised his hand, and his big face was solemn.

" Master," he said, relapsing into the vernacular in his excitement, " though this ki-chu lives in a village of devils, and ghosts walk about his hut, I will bring him."

The next morning Bosambo disappeared, taking with him three hunters of skill, and to those who met him and said, " Ho ! Bosambo ; where do you walk ? " he answered no word, but men who saw his face were shocked, for Bosambo had been a Christian and knew the value of money.

Eight days he was absent, and Big Ben Hold found life very pleasant, for he was treated with all the ceremony which is usually the privilege of kings.

On the evening of the eighth day Bosambo returned, and he brought with him the ki-chu.

Looking at this wonder Big Ben Hold found his heart beating faster.

" My God ! " he said, and his profanity was almost excusable.

For the ki-chu exceeded his wildest dreams. It was like a man, yet unlike. Its head was almost bald, the stick tied bit-wise between his teeth had been painted green and added to the sinister appearance of the brute. Its long arms reaching nearly to its knees were almost human, and the big splayed feet dancing a never-ceasing tattoo of rage were less than animal.

" Lord," said Bosambo proudly, " I have found the ki-chu ! "

The chief's face bore signs of a fierce encounter. It was gashed and lacerated. His arms, too, bore signs of rough surgical dressing.

" Three hunters I took with me," said Bosambo, " and one have I brought back, for I took the ki-chu as he sat on a tree, and he was very fierce."

" My God ! " said Big Ben again, and breathed heavily.

They built a cage for the ki-chu, a cage of heavy wooden bars, and the rare animal was screened from the vulgar gaze by curtains of native cloth.

It did not take kindly to its imprisonment.

It howled and gibbered and flung itself against the bars, and Bosambo viewed its transports with interest.

, " Lord," he said, " this only I ask you : that you take this ki-chu shortly from here. Also, you shall not show it to Sandi lest he be jealous that we send away from our country so rare a thing."

" But," protested Mr. Hold to the interpreter, " you tell the chief that Mr. Sanders just wants me to catch the ki-chu—say, Bosambo, you savee, Sandi wantee see dem ki-chu ? "

They were sitting before the chief's hut on the ninth day of the American's visit. The calm of evening lay on the city, and save for the unhappy noises of the captive no sound broke the Sabbath stillness of the closing day.

Bosambo was sitting at his ease, a bundle of English banknotes suspended by a cord about his neck, and the peace of heaven in his heart.

He had opened his mouth to explain the idio-syncrasies of the Commissioner when——

" Whiff—snick ! "

Something flicked past Big Ben's nose—something that buried its head in the straw of the hut with a soft swish !

He saw the quivering arrow, heard the shrill call of alarm and the dribbling roll of a skin-covered drum.

Then a hand like steel grasped his arm and flung him headlong into the hut, for Sakola's headman had come in person to avenge certain indignities and the city of the Ochori was surrounded by twenty thousand bushmen.

Night was falling and the position was desperate. Bosambo had no doubt as to that. A wounded bushman fell into his hands—a mad little man, who howled and spat and bit like a vicious little animal.

" Burn him till he talks," said Bosambo—but at the very sight of fire the little man told all—and Bosambo knew that he spoke the truth.

The *lokali* on the high watch tower of the city beat its staccato call for help and some of the villagers about answered.

Bosambo stood at the foot of the rough ladder leading to the tower, listening.

From east and south and north came the replies —from the westward—nothing. The bushmen had swept into the country from the west, and the *lokalis* were silent where the invader had passed.

Big Ben Hold, an automatic pistol in his hand,

took his part in the defence of the city. All through that night charge after charge broke before the defences, and at intervals the one firearm of the defending force spat noisily out into the darkness.

With the dawn came an unshaven Sanders. He swept round the bend of the river, two Hotchkiss guns banging destructively, and the end of the bush war came when the rallied villagers of the Ochori fell on the left flank of the attackers and drove them towards the guns of the *Zaire*.

Then it was that Bosambo threw the whole fighting force of the city upon the enemy.

Sanders landed his Houssas to complete the disaster; he made his way straight to the city and drew a whistling breath of relief to find Big Ben Hold alive, for Big Ben was a white man, and moreover a citizen of another land. The big man held out an enormous hand of welcome.

" Glad to see you," he said.

Sanders smiled.

" Found that ki-chu ? " he asked derisively, and his eyes rose incredulously at the other's nod.

" Here ! " said Mr. Hold triumphantly, and he drew aside the curtains of the cage.

It was empty.

" Hell ! " bellowed Big Ben Hold, and threw his helmet on the ground naughtily.

" There it is ! " He pointed across the open stretch of country which separated the city from the forest. A little form was running swiftly towards the woods. Suddenly it stopped, lifted something from the ground, and turned towards

F

the group. As its hands came up, Sergeant Abiboo of the Houssas raised his rifle and fired ; and the figure crumpled up.

" My ki-chu ! " wailed the showman, as he looked down at the silent figure.

Sanders said nothing. He looked first at the dead Sakola, outrageously kidnapped in the very midst of his people, then he looked round for Bosambo, but Bosambo had disappeared.

At that precise moment the latter was feverishly scraping a hole in the floor of his hut wherein to bank his ill-gotten reward.

CHAPTER X

THE CHILD OF SACRIFICE

OUT of the waste came a long, low wail of infinite weariness. It was like the cry of a little child in pain. The Government steamer was drifting at the moment. Her engine had stopped whilst the engineer repaired a float which had been smashed through coming in contact with a floating log.

Assistant-Commissioner Sanders, a young man in those days, bent his head, listening. Again the wail arose; this time there was a sob at the end of it. It came from a little patch of tall, coarse elephant grass near the shore.

Sanders turned to his orderly.

" Take a canoe, O man," he said in Arabic, " and go with your rifle." He pointed. " There you will find a monkey that is wounded. Shoot him, that he may suffer no more, for it is written, ' Blessed is he that giveth sleep from pain.' "

Obedient to his master's order, Abiboo leapt into a little canoe, which the *Zaire* carried by her side, and went paddling into the grass.

He disappeared, and they heard the rustle of elephant grass; but no shot came.

They waited until the grass rattled again, and

Abiboo reappeared with a baby boy in the crook of his arm, naked and tearful.

This child was a first-born, and had been left on a sandy spit so that a crocodile might come and complete the sacrifice.

This happened nearly twenty years ago, and the memory of the drastic punishment meted out to the father of that first-born is scarcely a memory.

" We will call this child ' N'mika,' " Sanders had said, which means " the child of sacrifice."

N'mika was brought up in the hut of a good man, and came to maturity.

*   *   *   *

When the monkeys suddenly changed their abiding-place from the little woods near by Bonganga, on the Isisi, to the forest which lies at the back of the Akasava, all the wise men said with one accord that bad fortune was coming to the people of Isisi.

N'mika laughed at these warnings, for he was in Sanders's employ, and knew all things that happened in his district.

Boy and man he served the Government faith-fully ; loyalty was his high fetish, and Sanders knew this.

The Commissioner might have taken this man and made him a great chief ; and had N'mika raised the finger of desire, Sanders would have placed him above all others of his people ; but the man knew where he might serve best, and at nineteen he had scotched three wars, saved the life of Sanders twice, and had sent three petty chiefs of enterprising character to the gallows.

Then love came to N'mika.

He loved a woman of the Lesser Isisi—a fine, straight girl, and very beautiful by certain standards. He married her, and took her to his hut, making her his principal wife, and investing her with all the privileges and dignity of that office.

Kira, as the woman was called, was, in many ways, a desirable woman, and N'mika loved her as only a man of intelligence could love her · and she had ornaments of brass and of beads exceeding in richness the possessions of any other woman in the village.

Now, there are ways of treating a woman the world over, and they differ in very little degree whether they are black or white, cannibal or vegetarian, rich or poor.

N'mika treated this woman too well. He looked in the forest for her wishes, as the saying goes, and so insistent was this good husband on serving his wife, that she was hard put to it to invent requirements.

" Bright star reflected in the pool of the world," he said to her one morning, " what is your need this day ? Tell me, so that I may go and seek fulfilment."

She smiled. " Lord," she said, " I desire the tail of a white antelope."

" I will find this tail," he said stoutly, and went forth to his hunting, discouraged by the knowledge that the white antelope is seen once in the year, and then by chance.

Now this woman, although counted cold by many

former suitors, and indubitably discovered so by her husband, had one lover who was of her people, and when the seeker of white antelope tails had departed she sent a message to the young man.

That evening Sanders was " tied up " five miles from the village, and was watching the sun sinking in the swamp which lay south and west of the anchorage, when N'mika came down river in his canoe, intent on his quest, but not so intent that he could pass his lord without giving him due obeisance.

" Ho, N'mika ! " said Sanders, leaning over the rail of the boat, and looking down kindly at the solemn figure in the canoe, " men up and down the river speak of you as the wonderful lover."

" That is true, lord," said N'mika simply ; " for, although I paid two thousand matakos for this woman, I think she is worth more rods than have ever been counted."

Sanders nodded, eyeing him thoughtfully, for he suspected the unusual whenever women came into the picture, and was open to the conviction that the man was mad.

" I go now, lord, to serve her," N'mika said, and he played with one of the paddles with some embarrassment ; " for my wife desires a tail of a white antelope, and there is no antelope nearer than the N'gombi country—and white antelopes are very little seen."

Sanders's eyebrows rose.

" For many months," continued N'mika, " I must ek my beautiful white swish ; but I am pleased, finding happiness in weariness because I serve her."

Sanders made a sign, and the man clambered on deck.

"You have a powerful ju-ju," he said, when N'mika stood before him, "for I will save you all weariness and privation. Three days since I shot a white antelope on the edge of the Mourning Pools, and you shall be given its tail."

Into the hands of the waiting man he placed the precious trophy, and N'mika sighed happily.

"Lord," he said simply, "you are as a god to me—and have been for all time ; for you found me, and named me the 'Child of Sacrifice,' and I hope, my fine master, to give my life in your service. This would be a good end for me."

"This is a little thing, N'mika," said Sanders gently ; "but I give you now a greater thing, which is a word of wisdom. Do not give all your heart to one woman, lest she squeeze it till you are dead."

"That also would be a great end," said N'mika and went his way.

It was a sad way, for it led to knowledge.

Sanders was coming up the river at his leisure. Two days ahead of him had gone a canoe, swiftly paddled, to summon to the place of snakes, near the elephants' ground where three small rivers meet (it was necessary to be very explicit in a country which abounded in elephants' playgrounds and haunts of snakes, and was, moreover, watered by innumerable rivers), a palaver of the chiefs of his land.

To the palaver in the snake-place came the chiefs, high and puisne, the headmen, great and small, in their various states. Some arrived in war canoes, with *lokali* shrilling, announcing the dignity and pride of the lazy figure in the stern. Some came in patched canoes that leaked continually. Some tramped long journeys through the forest—Isisi, Ochori, Akasava, Little N'gombi and Greater Isisi. Even the shy bushmen came sneaking down the river, giving a wide berth to all other peoples, and grasping in their delicate hands spears and arrows which, as a precautionary measure, had been poisoned with tetanus.

Egili of the Akasava, Tombolo of the Isisi, N'rambara of the N'gombi, and, last but not least, Bosambo of the Ochori, came, the last named being splendid to behold; for he had a robe of green velvet, sent to him from the Coast, and about his neck, suspended by a chain, jewelled at intervals with Parisian diamonds, was a large gold-plated watch, with a blue enamel dial, which he consulted from time to time with marked insolence.

They sat upon their carved stools about the Commissioner, and he told them many things which they knew, and some which they had hoped he did not know.

" Now, I tell you," said Sanders, " I call you together because there is peace in the land, and no man's hand is against his brother's, and thus it has been for nearly twelve moons, and behold ! you all grow rich and fat."

" Kwai ! " murmured the chiefs approvingly.

"Therefore," said Sanders, "I have spoken a good word to Government for you, and Government is pleased ; also my King and yours has sent you a token of his love, which he has made with great mystery and intelligence, that you may see him always with you, watching you."

He had brought half a hundred oleographs of His Majesty from the headquarters, and these he had solemnly distributed. It was a head-and-shoulder photograph of the King lighting a cigarette, and had been distributed gratis with an English Christmas number.

"Now all people see ! For peace is a beautiful thing, and men may lie down in their huts and fear nothing of their using. Also, they may go out to their hunting and fear nothing as to their return, for their wives will be waiting with food in their hands."

"Lord," said a little chief of the N'gombi, "even I, a blind and ignorant man, see all this. Now, I swear by death that I will hold the King's peace in my two hands, offending none ; for though my village is a small one, I have influence, owing to my wife's own brother, by the same father and of the same mother, being the high chief of the N'gombi-by-the-River."

"Lord Sandi," said Bosambo, and all eyes were fixed upon a chief so brave and so gallantly arrayed, who was, moreover, by all understanding, related too nearly to Sandi for the Commissioner's ease. "Lord Sandi," said Bosambo, "that I am your faithful slave all men know. Some have spoken

evilly of me, but, lo! where are they? They
are in hell, as your lordship knows, for we were
both Christians before I learnt the true way and
worshipped God and the Prophet. Nevertheless,
lord, Mussulman and Christian are one alike in
this, that they have a very terrible hell to which
their enemies go——"

"Bosambo," said Sanders interrupting, "your
voice is pleasant, and like the falling of rain after
drought, yet I am a busy man, and there are many
to speak."

Bosambo inclined his head gravely. The conference looked at him now in awe, for he had earned
an admonition from Sandi, and still lived—nay!
still preserved his dignity.

"Lord," said Bosambo. "I speak no more now,
for, as you say, we have many private palavers,
where much is said which no man knows; therefore it is unseemly to stand between other great
speakers and your honour." He sat down.

"You speak truly, Bosambo," said Sanders
calmly. "Often we speak in private, you and I,
for when I speak harshly to chiefs it is thus—in
the secrecy of their huts that I talk, lest I put
shame upon them in the eyes of their people."

"O, ko!" said the dismayed Bosambo under
his breath, for he saw the good impression his
cryptic utterance had wrought wearing off with
some rapidity.

After the palaver had dispersed, a weary Sanders
made his way to the *Zaire*. A bath freshened
him, and he came out to a wire-screened patch

of deck to his dinner with some zest. A chicken of microscopic proportions had been the main dish every night for months.

He ate his meal in solitude, a book propped up against a bottle before him, a steaming cup of tea at one elbow, and a little electric hand-lamp at the other.

He was worried. For nine months he had kept a regiment of the Ochori on the Isisi border prepared for any eventualities. This regiment had been withdrawn. Sanders had an uncomfortable feeling that he had made a bad mistake. It would take three weeks to police the border again.

Long after the meal had been cleared away he sat thinking, and then a familiar voice, speaking with Abiboo on the lower deck, aroused him.

He turned to the immobile Houssa orderly who squatted outside the fly wire.

"If that voice is the voice of the chief Bosambo, bring him to me."

A minute later Bosambo came, standing before the meshed door of the fly-proof enclosure.

"Enter, Bosambo," said Sanders, and when he had done so: "Bosambo," he said, "you are a wise man, though somewhat boastful. Yet I have some faith in your judgment. Now you have heard all manner of people speaking before me, and you know that there is peace in this land. Tell me, by your head and your love, what things are there which may split this friendship between man and man ? "

"Lord," said Bosambo, preparing to orate at

length, " I know of two things which may bring
war, and the one is land and such high matters as
fishing rights and hunting grounds, and the other
is women. And, lord, since women live and are
born to this world every hour of the day, faster—
as it seems to me—than they die, there will always
be voices to call spears from the roof."

Sanders nodded. " And now ? " he asked.

Bosambo looked at him swiftly. " Lord," he
said suavely, " all men live in peace, as your
lordship has said this day, and we love one another
too well to break the King's peace. Yet we keep a
regiment of my Ochori on the Akasava border to
keep the peace."

" And now ? " said Sanders again, more softly.

Bosambo shifted uncomfortably. " I am your
man," he said, " I have eaten your salt, and have
shown you by various heroic deeds, and by terrible
fighting, how much I love you, lord Sandi."

" Yet," said Sanders, speaking rather to the
swaying electric bulb hanging from the awning,
" and yet I did not see the chief of the little Isisi
at my palaver."

Bosambo was silent for a moment. Then he
heaved a deep sigh.

" Lord," he said, with reluctant admiration,
" you have eyes all over your body. You can see
the words of men before they are uttered, and are
very quick to read thoughts. You are all eyes,"
he went on extravagantly, " you have eyes on the
top of your head and behind your ears. You have
eyes——"

"That will do," said Sanders quietly. "I think that will do, Bosambo."

There was another long pause.

"And I tell you this, because there are no secrets between you and me. It was I who persuaded the little chief not to come."

Sanders nodded. "That I know," he said.

"For, lord, I desired that this should be a very pleasant day for your lordship, and that you should go away with your heart filled with gladness, singing great songs; also, as your lordship knows, the Ochori guard has left the Akasava border."

There was no mistaking the significance.

"Why should Bimebibi make me otherwise?" asked Sanders, ignoring the addition.

"Lord," said Bosambo loftily, "I am, as you know, of the true faith, believing neither in devils nor spells, save those which are prescribed by the blessed Prophet. It is well known that Bimebibi is a friend of ghosts, and has the eye which withers and kills. Therefore, lord, he is an evil man, and all the chiefs and peoples of this land are for chopping him—all save the people of the Lesser Isisi, who greatly love him."

Again Sanders nodded.

The Lesser Isisi were the fighting Isisi; they held the land between the Ochori and the Akasava, and were fierce men in some moments, though gentle enough in others. Yet he had had no word from N'mika that trouble was brewing. This was strange. Sanders sat in thought for the greater part of ten minutes. Then he spoke.

" War is very terrible," he said, " for if one mad man comes up against five men who are not mad, behold ! they become all mad together. I tell you this, Bosambo, if you do well for me in this matter, I will pay you beyond your dreams."

" How can a man do well ? " asked Bosambo.

" He shall hold this war," said Sanders.

Bosambo raised his right arm stiffly.

" This I would do, lord," he said gravely ; " but it is not for me, for Bimebibi will cross with the Akasava just as soon as he knows that the Ochori do not hold the border."

" He must never know until I bring my soldiers," said Sanders ; " and none can tell him." He looked up quietly, and met the chief's eye. " And none can tell him ? " he challenged.

Bosambo shook his head. " N'mika sits in his village, lord," said he ; " and N'mika is a great lover of his wife by all accounts."

Sanders smiled. " If N'mika betrays me," he said, " there is no man in the world I will ever trust."

*   *   *   *

N'mika faced his wife. He wore neither frown nor smile, but upon her face was the terror of death. On a stool in the centre of the hut was the tail of the white antelope, but to this she gave no attention, for her mind was busy with the thoughts of terrible reprisals.

They sat in silence ; the fire in the centre of the big hut spluttered and burnt, throwing weird shadows upon the wattle walls.

When N'mika spoke his voice was even and calm.

"Kira, my wife," he said, "you have taken my heart out of me, and left a stone, for you do not love me."

She licked her dry lips and said nothing.

"Now, I may put you away," he went on, "for the shame you have brought, and the sorrow, and the loneliness."

She opened her mouth to speak. Twice she tried, but her tongue refused. Then, again:

"Kill me," she whispered, and kept her staring eyes on his.

N'mika, the Wonderful Lover, shook his head.

"You are a woman, and you have not my strength," he said, half to himself, "and you are young. I have trusted you, and I am afraid."

She was silent.

If the man, her lover, did what she had told him to do in the frantic moment when she had been warned of her husband's return, she might have saved her life—and more.

He read her thoughts in part.

"You shall take no harm from me," he said; "for I love you beyond understanding; and though I stand on the edge of death for my kindness, I will do no ill to you."

She sprang up. The fear in her eyes was gone; hate shone there banefully. He saw the look, and it scorched his very soul—and he heard.

It was the soft pad-pad of the king's guard, and he turned to greet Bimebibi's head chief.

His wife would have run to the guard, but N'mika's hand shot out and held her.

"Take him—take him!" she cried hoarsely "He will kill me—also he plots against the king, for he is Sandi's man!"

Chekolana, the king's headman, watched her curiously, but no more dispassionate was the face her husband turned upon her.

"Kira," he said, "though you hate me, I love you. Though I die for this at the hands of the king, I love you."

She laughed aloud.

She was safe—and N'mika was afraid. Her outstretched finger almost touched his face.

"Tell this to the king," she cried, "N'mika is Sandi's man, and knows his heart——"

The headman, Chekolana, made a step forward and peered into N'mika's face.

"If this is true," he said, "you shall tell Bime-bibi all he desires to know. Say, N'mika, how many men of the Ochori hold the border?"

N'mika laughed.

"Ask Sandi that," he said.

"Lord! lord!"—it was the woman, her eyes blazing—"this I will tell you, if you put my man away. On the border there is——"

She gasped once and sighed like one grown weary, then she slid down to the floor of the hut—dead, for N'mika was a quick killer, and his hunting-knife very sharp.

"Take me to the king," he said, his eyes upon the figure at his feet, " saying N'mika has slain the woman he loved ; N'mika, the Wonderful Lover ; N'mika, the Child of Sacrifice, who loved his wife well, and loved his high duty best."

No other word spoke N'mika.

They crucified him on a stake before the chief's hut, and there Sanders found him three days later, Bimebibi explained the circumstances.

" Lord, this man murdered a woman, so I killed him," he said.

He might have saved his breath, for he had need of it.

CHAPTER XI

" THEY "

IN the Akarti country they worshipped many devils, and feared none, save one strange devil, who was called "Wu," which in our language means " They."

" Remember this," said Sanders of the River, as he grasped the hand of Grayson Smith, his assistant.

" I will not forget," said that bright young man ; " and, by the way, if anything happens to me, you might find out how it all came about, and drop a note to my people—suppressing the beastly details."

Sanders nodded.

" I will make it a pretty story," he said ; " and, whatever happens, your death will be as instantaneous and as painless as my fountain-pen can make it."

" You're a brick ! " said Grayson Smith, and turned to swear volubly in Swaheli at his headman —for Smith, albeit young, was a great linguist.

Sanders watched the big canoe as it swung

into the yellow waters of the Fasai; watched it until it disappeared round a bank, then sent his steamer round to the current, and set his course homeward.

To appreciate the full value of the Akartis' independence, and their immunity from all attack, it must be remembered that the territory ranged from the Forest-by-the-Waters to the Forest-by-the-Mountains. It was a stretch of broad, pastoral lands, enclosed by natural defences. Forest and swamp on the westward kept back the rapacious people of the Great King, mountain and forest on the south held the Ochori, the Akasava, and the Isisi.

The boldest of the N'gombi never ventured across the saw-shaped peaks of the big mountains, even though loot and women were there for the taking.

The king of the Akarti was undisputed lord of vast territories, and he had ten regiments of a thousand men, and one regiment of women, whom he called his " Angry Maidens," who drank strong juices, and wrestled like men.

Since he was king from the Forest-by-the-Mountains to the Forest-by-the-Waters he was powerful and merciless, and none said " nay " to N'raki's " yea," for he was too fierce, and too terrible a man to cross.

Culuka of the Wet Lands once came down into N'raki's territory, and brought a thousand spears.

Now the Wet Lands are many miles from the city of the king, and the raid that Culuka planned injured none, for the raided territories were poor and stony.

But N'raki, the killer, was hurt in his tenderest spot, and he led his thousands across the swamps to the city of Culuka, and he fought him up to the stockades and beyond. The city he burnt. The men and children he slew out of hand. Culuka he crucified before his flaming hut, and, thereafter, the borders of the killer were immune from attack.

This was a lesson peculiarly poignant, and when the French Government—for Culuka dwelt in a territory which was nominally under the tricolour—sent a mission to inquire into the wherefores of the happening, N'raki cut off the head of the leader, and sent it back with unprintable messages intended primarily for the governor of French West Africa, and eventually for the Quai d'Orsay.

N'raki lived, therefore, undisturbed, for the outrage coincided with the findings of the Demarcation Commission which had been sitting for two years to settle certain border-line questions. By the finding of the Commission all the Akarti country became, in the twinkling of an eye, British territory, and N'raki a vassal of the King of England —though he was sublimely unconscious of the honour.

N'raki was an autocrat of autocrats, and of his many battalions of skilled fighting men, all very young and strong, with shining limbs and feathered heads, he was proudest of his first regiment.

These were the tallest, the strongest, the fleetest, and the fiercest of fighters, and he forbade them to marry, for all men know that women have an evil effect upon warriors; and no married man is brave until he has children to defend, and by that time he is fat also.

So this austere regiment knew none of the comforts or languor of love, and they were proud that their lord, the king, had set them apart from all other men, and had so distinguished them.

At the games they excelled, because they were stronger and faster, knowing nothing of women's influence; and the old king saw their excellence, and said " Wa ! "

There was a man of the regiment whose name was Taga'ka, who was a fine man of twenty. There was also in the king's city a woman of fifteen, named Lapai, who was a straight, comely girl, and a great dancer.

She was a haughty woman, because her uncle was the chief witch-doctor, and such was her power that she had put away two husbands.

One day, at the wells, she saw Taga'ka, and loved him ; and meeting him alone in the forest, she fell down before him and clasped his feet.

" Lord Taga'ka," said she, " you are the one man in the world I desire."

" I am beyond desire," said Taga'ka, in his arrogant pride; " for I am of the king's regiment, and women are grass for our feet."

And not all her allurements could tempt him

to so much as stroke her face; and the heart of the woman was wild with grief.

Then the king fell sick, and daily grew worse.

The witch-doctors made seven sacrifices, and learnt from grisly portents, which need not be described in detail, that the king should take a long journey to the far end of his kingdom, where he should meet a man with one eye, who would live in the shadow of the royal hut.

This he did, journeying for three months, till he came to the appointed place, where he met a man afflicted in accordance with the prediction. And the man sat in the shadow of the king's hut.

Now, it is a fact, which none will care to deny, that the niece of the chief witch-doctor had planned the treatment of the king. She had planned it with great cleverness, and she it was who saw to it that the deformed man waited at the king's hut.

For she loved Taga'ka with all the passion of her soul, and when the long months passed, and the king remained far away, and Lapai whispered into the young man's ear, he took her to wife, though death would be his penalty for his wrong-doing.

The other men of the royal regiment, who held Taga'ka a model in all things austere, seeing this happen, said: "Behold! Taga'ka, the favourite of the king, has taken a woman to himself. Now, if we all do this, it would be better for Taga'ka, and better for us. The king, the old man, will forgive him, and not punish us."

It might have been that N'raki, the king, would

have ended his days in the place to which his medicine-man had sent him, but there arose in that district a greater magician than any—a certain wild alien of the Wet Lands, who possessed magical powers, and cured pains in the king's legs by a no more painful process than the laying on of hands, and whom the king appointed his chief magician. And this was the end of the uncle of Lapai ; for, if no two kings can rule in one land, most certainly no two witch-doctors can hold power.

And they killed the deposed uncle of Lapai, and used the blood for making spells.

One morning the new witch-doctor stood in the presence of N'raki the king.

"Lord king," he said, "I have had a dream, and it says that your lordship shall go back to your city, and that you shall travel secretly, so that the devils who guard the way shall not lay hands upon you."

N'raki, the king, went back to his city unattended, save by his personal guard, and unheralded, to the discomfort of the royal regiment.

And when he learnt what he learnt, he administered justice swiftly. He carried the forbidden wives to the top of a high mountain and cast them over a cliff, one by one, to the number of six hundred.

And that mountain is to this day called "The Mountain of Sorrowful Women."

One alone he spared—Lapai. Before the assembled people in judgment he spared her.

" Behold this woman, people of the Akarti !"
he said ; " she that has brought sorrow and death
to my regiment. To-day she shall watch her
man, Taga'ka, burn ; and from henceforth she shall
live amongst you to remind you that I am a very
jealous king, and terrible in my anger."

The news of the massacre filtered slowly through
the territories. It came to the British Government,
but the British Government is a cautious Government where primitive natives are concerned.

Sanders, sitting between Downing Street and the
District Commissioners of many far-away and
isolated spots, realised the futility of an expedition. He sent two special messages, one of which
was to a young man named Farquharson, who,
at the moment, was shooting snipe on the big
swamp south of the Ambalina Mountains. And
this young man swore like a Scotsman because
his sport had been interrupted, but girded up his
loins, and, with half a company of the King's
African Rifles, trekked for the city.

On his way he ran into an ambush, and swore
still more, for he realised that death had over-
taken him before he had had his annual holiday.

He called for his orderly.

" Hafiz," he said in Arabic, " if you should
escape, cross the country to the Ochori land by
the big river There you will find Sandi ; give
him my dear love, and say that Fagozoni sent a
cheerful word, also that the Slayer of Regiments
is killing his people."

An hour later Farquharson, or Fagozoni, as

they called him, was lying before the king, his
unseeing eyes staring at the hard, blue heavens,
his lips parted in the very ghost of a smile.
" This is a bad palaver," said the king, looking
at the dead man. " Now they will come, and I
know not what will happen."

In his perturbation he omitted to take into his
calculations the fact that he had in his city a thous-
and men sick with grief at the loss of their wives.

N'raki, the king, was no coward. There was a
prompt smelling out of all suspicious characters.
Even the councillors about his person were not
exempt, for the new witch-doctor found traces of
disloyalty in every one.

With the aid of his regiment of virgins, he held
his city, and ruthlessly disposed of secret critics.
These included men who stood at his very elbow,
and there came a time when he found none to whom
he might transmit his thoughts with any feeling
of security.

News came to him that there was an Arab caravan traversing his western border, trading with his
people, and the report he received was flattering
to the intelligence and genius of the man in charge
of the party.

N'raki sent messengers with gifts and kind
words to the intruder, and on a certain day there
was brought before him the slim Arab, Ussuf.

" O Ussuf," said the king, " I have heard of you,
and of your wisdom. Often you have journeyed
through my territories, and no man has done you
hurt."

" Lord king," said the Arab, " that is true."

The king looked at him thoughtfully. N'raki, in those days, had reached his maturity ; he was a wise, cunning man, and had no illusions.

" Arabi," he said, " this is in my mind : that you shall stay here with me, living in the shadow of my hut, and be my chief man, for you are very clever, and know the ways of foreign people. You shall have treasures beyond your dreams, for in this land there is much dead ivory hidden by the people of my fathers."

" Lord king," said Ussuf, " this is a very great honour, and I am too mean and small a man to serve you. Yet it is true I know the ways of foreign people, and I am wise in the government of men."

" This also I say to you," the king went on slowly, " that I do not fear men or devils, yet I fear ' They,' because of their terrible cruelty. Now if you will serve me, so that I avert the wrath of these, you shall sit down here in peace and happiness."

Thus it came about that Ussuf, the Arab, became Prime Minister to the King of Akarti, and two days after his arrival the new witch-doctor was put away with promptitude and dispatch by a king who had no further use for him.

All the news that came from the territories to Sanders was that the country was being ruled with some wisdom. The fear of " They " was an ever-present fear with the king. The long evenings he sat with his Arab counsellor, thinking

of that mysterious force which lay beyond the
saw-back.

"I tell you this, Ussuf," he said, "that my heart
is like water within me when I think of 'They,'
for it is a terrible devil, and I make sacrifices at
every new moon to appease its anger."

"Lord king," said Ussuf, "I am skilled in the
way of 'They,' and I tell you that they do not
love sacrifices."

The king shifted on his stool irritably.

"That is strange," he said, "for the gods told
me in a dream that I must sacrifice Lapai."

He shot a swift glance at the Arab, for this Ussuf
was the only man in the city who did not deal
scornfully with the lonely, outcast woman, whose
every day was a hell.

It was the king's order that she should walk
through the city twice between sunrise and sunset, and it was the king's pleasure that every man
she met should execrate her; and although the
native memory is short, and the recollection of
the tragedy had died, men feared the king too much
to allow her to pass without a formal curse.

Ussuf alone had walked with her, and men had
gasped to see the kindly Arabi at her side.

"You may have this woman," said the king
suddenly, "and take her into your house."

The Arab turned his calm eyes upon the wizened
face of the other.

"Lord," he said, "she is not of my faith, being
an unbeliever and an infidel, and, according to my
gods, unworthy."

He was wise to the danger his undiplomatic friendship had brought him. He knew the reigns of Prime Ministers were invariably short.

He had become less indispensable than he had been, for the king had regained some of his lost confidence in the loyalty of his people; moreover, he had aroused suspicion in the Akartis' mind, and that was fatal.

The king dismissed him, and Ussuf went back to his hut, where his six Arab followers were.

" Ahmed," he said to one of these, " it is written in the blessed Word that the life of man is very short. Now I particularly desire that it shall be no shorter than the days our God has given to me. Be prepared to-morrow, therefore, to leave this city, for I see an end to my power."

He rose early in the morning, and went to the palaver which began the day. He was not perturbed to discover the seat usually reserved on the right of the king occupied by a lesser chief, and his own stool placed four seats down on the left.

" I have spoken with my wise counsellors," said the king, " also with witch-doctors, and these wise men have seen that the crops are bad, and that there is no fortune in this land, and because of this we will make a great sacrifice."

Ussuf bowed his head.

" Now, I think," said King N'raki slowly, " because I love my people very dearly, and I will not take any young maidens, as is the custom, for the fire, and for the killing, that it would be good for all people if I took the woman Lapai."

All eyes were fixed on Ussuf. His face was calm and motionless.

" Also," the king went on, " I hear terrible things, which fill my stomach with sorrow."

" Lord, I hear many things also," said Ussuf calmly ; " but I am neither sorry nor glad, for such stories belong to the women at their cooking-pots and to men who are mad because of sickness."

N'raki made a little face.

" Women or madmen," he said shortly, " they say that you are under the spell of this woman, and that you are plotting against this land, and have also sent secret messengers to ' They,' and that you will bring great armies against my warriors, eating up my country as Sandi ate up the Akasava and the lands of the Great King."

Ussuf said nothing. He would not deny this for many reasons.

" When the moon comes up," said the king, and he addressed the assembly generally, " you shall tie Lapai to a stake before my royal house, and all the young maidens shall dance and sing songs, for good fortune will come to us, as it came in the days of my father, when a bad woman died."

Ussuf made no secret of his movements that day. First he went to his hut at the far end of the village, and spoke to the six Arabs who had come with him into the kingdom.

To the headman he said ·

" Ahmed, this is a time when death is very near us all, be ready at moonrise to die, if needs be. But since life is precious to us all, be at the little plantation at the edge of the city at sunset, as soon as darkness falls and the people come in to sacrifice."

He left them and walked through the broad, palm-fringed street of the Akarti city till he came to the lonely hut, where the outcast woman dwelt. It was such a hut as the people of Akarti built for those who are about to die, so that no dwelling-place might be polluted with the mustiness of death.

The girl was starting on her daily penance—a tall, fine woman. She watched the approach of the king's minister without expressing in her face any of the torments which raged in her bosom.

" Lapai," said Ussuf, " this night the king makes a sacrifice."

He made no further explanation, nor did the girl require one.

" If he had made this sacrifice earlier, he would have been kind," she said quietly, " for I am a very sorrowful woman."

" That I know, Lapai," said the Arab gently.

" That you do not know," she corrected. " I had sorrow because I loved a man and destroyed him, because I love my people and they hate me, and now because I love you, Ussuf, with a love which is greater than any."

He looked at her ; there was a strange pity in his eyes, and his thin, brown hands went out till they reached to her shoulders.

" All things are with the gods," he said. " Now, I cannot love you, Lapai, although I am full of pity for you, for you are not of my race, and there are other reasons. But because you are a woman, and because of certain teachings which I received in my youth, I will take you out of this city, and, if needs be, die for you."

He watched her as she walked slowly down towards where the people of the Akarti waited for her, drawn by morbid curiosity, since the king's intention was no secret. Then he shrugged his shoulders helplessly.

At nine o'clock, when the virgin guards and the old king went to find her for the killing, she had gone.

So also had Ussuf and his six Arabi. The king's *lokali* beat furiously, summoning all the country to deliver into his hands the woman and the man.

*   *   *   *

Sanders, at that moment, was hunting for the Long Man, whose name was O'Fasa. O'Fasa was twelve months gone in sleeping-sickness, and had turned from being a gentle husband and a kindly father into a brute beast. He had speared his wife, cut down the Houssa guard left by Sanders to keep the peace of his village, and had made for the forest.

Now, a madman is a king, holding his subjects in the thrall of fear, and since there was no room in the territory for two kings and Sanders, the Commissioner came full tilt up the river, landed half a company of black infantry, and followed on the ravaging trace of the madman.

At the end of eight days he came upon O'Fasa,

the Long Man. He was sitting with his back
against a gum-tree, his well-polished spears close
at hand, and he was singing the death song of the
Isisi, a long low, wailing, sorrowful song, which
may be so translated into doggerel English :

> Life is a thing so small
> That you cannot see it at all;
> Death is a thing so wise
> That you see it in every guise.
> Death is the son of life,
> Pain is his favourite wife.

Sanders went slowly across the clearing, his automatic pistol in his hand.

O'Fasa looked at him and laughed.

" O'Fasa," said Sanders gently, " I have come
to see you, because my King heard you were sick."

" O ko ! " laughed the other. " I am a great
man when kings send their messengers to me."

Sanders, his eye upon the spears, advanced
warily.

" Come with me, O'Fasa," he said.

The man rose to his feet. He made no attempt
to reach his spears. Of a sudden he ducked, and
turned, running swiftly towards the black heart
of the forest. Sanders raised his pistol, and hesitated a second—just too long. He could not kill
the man, though by letting him live he might en-
danger the lives of his fellows and the peace of
the land.

The Commissioner was in an awkward predica
ment. Ten miles beyond was the narrow gap
which led into the territory of N'raki. To lead

an armed expedition through that gap would bring about complications which it was his duty and desire to avoid. The only hope was that O'Fasa would double back, for the trail they followed left little doubt as to where he had gone Unerringly, with the instinct of the hunted beast, he had made for the gap.

They came to the gorge, palm-fringed, and damp with the running waters, at sunset, and camped. They found the spoor of the hunted man, lost it, and picked it up again. At daybreak Sanders, with two men, pushed through the narrow pass and came into the forbidden territory. There was no sign of the fugitive.

Sanders's *lokali* beat out four urgent messages. They were addressed to a Mr. Grayson Smith, who might possibly be in that neighbourhood, but if he received them, he sent no reply.

Now, madmen and children have a rooted dislike for strange places, and Sanders, backing on this, fixed his ambush in the narrow end of the gorge. Sooner or later O'Fasa would return. At any rate, he decided to give him four days.

Thus matters stood when the sometime minister, Ussuf, with a woman and five Arabi, made for the gap, with the swift and tireless guards of the king at their heels.

Three times the Arab had halted to fight off his -pursuers, and in one of these engagements he had sustained his only casualty, and had left a dead Arab follower on the ground of his stand.

The gap was in sight, when a regiment of the

north, summoned by *lokali*, swept down on his left and effectively blocked his retreat. Ussuf took up his position on a little rocky hill. His right was protected by swamp land, and his left and rear were open.

"Lapai," he said, when he had surveyed the position, " it seems to me that the death you desire is very close at hand. Now, I am very sorry for you, but God knows my sorrow can do little to save you."

The woman looked at him steadily.

" Lord," she said, " I am very glad if you and I go down to hell together, for in some new, strange world you might love me, and I should be satisfied."

Ussuf laughed, showing his straight rows of white teeth in genuine amusement.

" That we shall see," he said.

The attack came almost at once, but the rifles of the six shot back the assault. At the end of two hours the little party stood intact. A second attack followed ; one man of the Arab guard went down with an arrow through his throat, but Ussuf's shooting was effective, and again the northern regiment drew off.

Before the hill, and in the direction of Akarti city, was the king's legion. It was from this point that Ussuf expected the last destroying assault.

" Lapai," he said, turning round, " I——"

The woman had gone ! In the fury of the defence he had not noticed her slip away from him. Suddenly she appeared half-way down the hill and turned to him.

" Come back ! " he called.

She framed her mouth with two hands that her words might carry better. In the still evening air every word came distinctly.

" Lord," she said, " this is best, for if they have me, they will let you go, and death will come some day to you, and I shall be waiting."

She turned and ran quickly down the hill towards the stiff lines of warriors below.

Then suddenly appeared out of the ground, as it seemed, a tall, lank figure right in her path. She stopped a moment, and the man sprang at her and lifted her without an effort. Ussuf raised his rifle and covered them, but he dare not shoot.

There was another interested spectator. King N'raki, a vengeful man, and agile despite his years, had followed as eagerly as the youngest of his warriors, and now stood in the midst of his counsellors, watching the scene upon the hill.

" What man is that ? " he asked. " For I see he is not of our people."

Before the messengers he would have dispatched could be instructed, the tall man, running lightly with his burden, came towards him, and laid a dead woman almost at the king's feet.

" Man," he said insolently, " I bring you this woman, whom I have killed, because a devil put it into my heart to do so."

" Who are you ? " asked N'raki. " For I see you are a stranger."

" I am a king," said O'Fasa, the Long Man !

"greater than all kings, for I have behind me the armies of white men."

The humour of this twisted truth struck him of a sudden, for he burst into a fit of uncontrollable laughter.

"You have the armies of the white men behind you?" repeated N'raki slowly, and looked nervously from side to side.

"Behold!" said O'Fasa, stretching out his hand.

The king's eyes followed the direction of the hand. Far away across the bare plain he saw black specks of men advancing at regular intervals. The sinking sun set the bayonets of Sander's little force aglitter. The Commissioner had heard the firing, and had guessed much.

"It is 'They,'" said King N'raki, and blinked furiously at the Long Man, O'Fasa.

He turned swiftly to his guard.

"Kill that man!" he said.

*   *   *   *

Sanders brought his half-company of Houssas to the hill and was met half-way by Ussuf.

"I heard your rifles," he said. "Have you seen anything of a long chap, of wild and aggressive mien?" He spoke in English, and Ussuf replied in the same language.

"A tall man?" he asked, and Sanders wondered a little that a man so unemotional as was Grayson Smith, of the Colonial Intelligence, should speak so shakily.

"I think he is here," said the Englishman in Arab attire, and he led the way down the hill.

N'raki's armies had moved off swiftly. The fear of " They " had been greater in its effect than all its legions.

The Englishmen made their way to where two figures lay in a calm sleep of death.

" Who is the woman ? " asked Sanders.

" A native woman, who loved me," said Grayson Smith simply, and he bent down and closed the eyes of the girl who had loved him so well.

CHAPTER XII

THE AMBASSADORS

THERE is a saying amongst the Akasava:
"The Isisi sees with his eyes, the N'gombi
with his ears, but the Ochori sees nothing
but his meat."

This is translated badly, but in its original form
it is immensely subtle. In the old days before
Bosambo became chief, king, headman, or what
you will, of his people, the Ochori were quite prepared to accept the insulting description of their
sleepiness without resentment.

But this was *cala-cala*, and now the Ochori are
a proud people, and it is not good to throw insulting proverbs in their direction, lest they throw
them back with something good and heavy at the
end of it.

The native mind works slowly, and it was not
until every tribe within three hundred miles had
received some significant indication of the change
which had come about in the spirit and character
of this timorous people, that they realised the
Ochori were no longer a race which might serve
as butts for the shafts of wisdom.

There was a petty chief of the Isisi who governed a great district, for, although "Isisi" means "small" the name must not be taken literally. He had power under his king to call palavers on all great national questions, such as the failure of crops, the shifting of fishing-grounds, and the infidelities of highly-placed women.

One day he called his people together—his counsellors, his headmen, and all sons of chiefs—and he laid before them a remarkable proposition.

"In the days of my father," said Emberi, "the Ochori were a weak and cowardly people; now they have become strong and powerful. Last week they came down upon our brothers of the Akasava and stole their goats and laid shame upon them, and behold! the Akasava, who are great warriors, did nothing more than send to Sandi the story of their sorrow. Now it seems to me that this is because Bosambo, the chief, has a devil of great potency, and I have sent to my king to ask him to entreat the lord Bosambo to tell us why these things should be."

The gathered counsellors nodded their heads wisely. There was no doubt at all that Bosambo had the advantage of communication with a devil; or if this were not so, he was blessed to a minor degree with a nodding acquaintance with one of those ghosts in which the forest of the Ochori abounded.

"And thus says my lord, the king of the Akasava, and of all the territories and the rivers and the unknown lands beyond the forest as far as the eye can see," the chief went on. "He sends me his message by his counsellor, saying: 'It is true Bosambo has a devil, and for the sake of my people I will send to him, asking him to put his strength in our hands, that we may be wise and bold.'"

Now this was a conclusion which had been arrived at simultaneously by the six nations, and, although the thoughts of their rulers were not communicated in such a public fashion, the faith in Bosambo's inspiration was universal, and the idea that Bosambo should be thus approached was a violent and shameless plagiarism on the part of the chief Emberi.

One morning in the late spring the ambassadors of the powers came paddling up to Ochori city in twelve canoes with their headmen, their warriors, their beaters of drums and their carriers. Bosambo, who had no faith whatever in humanity, was warned of their approach and threw the city into a condition of defence. He himself received the deputation on the foreshore, and the spokesman was Emberi.

"Lord Bosambo," said the chief, "we come in peace, and from the chief and the kings and all the peoples of these lands."

"That may be so," said Bosambo, "and my heart is full of joy to see you. But I beg of you that you land your spearmen and your warriors and your beaters of drums on the other side of the river, for I am a timorous man, and I fear that I cannot in this city show you the love and honour which Sandi has asked me to give even to common people."

" But, lord," protested the chief, who, to do him credit, had no warlike or injurious ideas concerning his host, " on the other side of the water there is only sand and water and evil spirits."

" That may be so," said Bosambo ; " but on this side of the river there are me and my people, and we desire to live happily for many years. I tell you, that it is better that you should all die because of the sand and the water and the evil spirits, than that I should be slain by those who do not love me."

" My master," said Emberi pompously, " is a great king and a great lover of you."

" Your master," said Bosambo, " is a great liar."

" He loves you," protested Emberi.

" He is still a great liar," said Bosambo ; " for the last time I met him he not only said that he would come with his legions and eat me up, but he also called me evil names, such as ' fish-eater ' and ' chicken,' and ' fat dog.' "

Bosambo spoke without fear of consequences because he had a hundred of his picked men behind him, and all the advantage of the sloping beach. He would have turned the delegates back to their homes, but that the persistent and alarmed Emberi succeeded in interesting him in his announcements, and, more important, there were landed from one of the canoes, rich presents, including goats and rice and a looking-glass, which latter was, explained Emberi, the very core of his master's soul.

In the end Bosambo left his hundred men to

hold the beach, and Emberi persuaded his reluctant
followers to make their home on the sandy shore
across the river.

Then, and only then, did Bosambo unbend, and
had prepared one of his famous feasts, to which
all the chiefs of the land contributed in the shape
of meat and drink—all the chiefs, that is, except
Bosambo, who made a point of giving nothing
away to anybody in any circumstances.

The palaver that followed was very interesting,
indeed, to the chief of the Ochori. One by one,
from nine in the morning to four in the following
morning, the delegates spoke.

Much of their speeches dealt with the superlative
qualities which distinguished Bosambo's rule—
his magnificent courage, his noble generosity—
Bosambo glanced quickly round to see the faces
of the counsellors who had reluctantly provided
the feast—and to the future which awaited all
nations which imitated all his virtues.

" Lord, I speak the truth," said Emberi, " and
thus it runs that all people from the sea where
the river ends, to the leopard's mouth from whence
it has its source, know that you are familiar with
devils that give you courage and cunning and tell
you magic, so that you can make men from rats."

Bosambo nodded his head gravely.

" All this is true," he said. " I have several
devils, although I do not always use them. For,
as you know, I am a follower of a particular faith,
and was for one life-time a Christian, believing
in all manners of mysteries of which you know

nothing—Marki, Luki, and Johnny Baptist, who are not for you."

He looked round at the awed men and shook his head.

" Nor do you know of the wonders they worked, such as curing burns, and striking dead, and cutting ears. Now I know these things," he continued impressively. " therefore Sandi loves me, for he also is a God-man, and often comes to me to speak with him concerning these white men."

" Lord, what are devils ? " asked an impatient delegate.

" Of the devils," repeated Bosambo, " I have many."

He half closed his eyes and was silent for the space of two minutes. He gave the impression that he was counting his staff—and, indeed, this was the idea precisely that he wished to convey.

" O ko ! " said Emberi in a hushed voice. " If it is true, as you say it is, then our master desires that you shall send us one devil or two that we might be taught the peculiar manner of these wonderful ghosts."

Bosambo coughed, and glanced round at the sober faces of his advisers.

" I have many devils who serve me," he began. " There is one I know who is very small and has two noses—one before him and one behind—so that he may smell his enemy who stalks him. Also there is one who is so tall that the highest trees are grass to his feet. And another one who is green and walks upside down."

For an hour Bosambo orated at length on dæmono-
logy, even though he might never have known the
word. He drew on the misty depths of his imagination. He availed himself of every recollection
dealing with science. He spoke of ghosts who
were familiar friends, and came to his bidding
much in the same way that the civilised dog comes
to his master's whistle.

The delegates retired to their huts for the night
in a condition of panic when Bosambo informed
them that he had duly appointed a particular
brand of devil to serve their individual needs, and
protect them against the ills which the flesh is
heir to.

Now Ochori city and the Ochori nation had indeed
awakened from the spell of lethargy under the
beneficent and drastic government of Bosambo,
and it is known in the history of nations, however
primitive or however advanced they may be, that
no matter how excellent may be the changes effected
there will be a small but compact party who regard
the reformer as one who encumbers the earth.
Bosambo had of his own people a small but powerful
section who regarded all changes with horror, and
who saw in the new spirit which the chief had
infused into the Ochori, the beginning of the
end. This is a view which is not peculiar to the
Ochori.

There were old chiefs and headmen who remembered the fat and idle days which preceded the
upraising of Bosambo, who remembered how easy
it was to secure slave service, and, remembering

spoke of Bosambo with unkindness. The chief might have settled the matter of devils out of hand in his own way, and would, I doubt not, have sent away the delegation happily enough with such messages of the Koran as he could remember written on the paper Sanders had supplied him for official messages.

But it was not Bosambo's way, nor was it the way with the men with whom he had to deal to expedite important palavers. Normally, such a conference as was now assembled, would last at least three days and three nights. It seemed that it would last much longer, for Bosambo had troubles of his own.

At dawn on the morning following the arrival of the delegation, a dust-stained messenger, naked as he was born, came at a jog-trot and panting heavily from the bush road which leads to the Elivi, and without ceremony stood at the door of the royal hut.

" Lord Bosambo," said the messenger, " Ikifari, the chief of Elivi, brings his soldiers and headmen to the number of a thousand, for a palaver."

" What is in his heart ? " said Bosambo.

" Master," said the man, " this is in his heart ꞉ there shall be no roads in the Ochori, for the men of Elivi are crying out against the work. They desire to live in peace and comfort."

Bosambo had instituted a law of his own—with the full approval of Sanders—and it was that each district should provide a straight and well-made forest road from one city to another, and a great road which should lead from one district to its neighbour.

Unfortunately, every little tribe did not approach the idea with the enthusiasm which Bosambo himself felt, nor regard it with the approval which was offered to this most excellent plan by the King's Government.

For road-making is a bad business. It brings men out early in the morning, and keeps them working with the sweat running off their bare backs in the hot hours of the day. Also there were fines and levies which Bosambo the chief took an unholy joy in extracting whenever default was made.

Of all the reluctant tribes, the Elivi were the most frankly so. Whilst all the others were covered with a network of rough roads—slovenly made, but roads none the less—Elivi stood a virgin patch of land two hundred miles square in the very heart of make-shift civilisation.

Bosambo might deal drastically with the enemy who stood outside his gate. It was a more delicate matter when he had to deal with a district tacitly rebellious, and this question of roads threatened to develop, unhappily.

He had sent spies into the land of the Elivi and this was the first man back.

" Now it seems to me," said Bosambo, half to himself, " that I have need of all my devils, for Ikifari is a bitter man, and his sons and his counsellors are of a mind with him."

He sent his headman to his guests with a message

that for the whole day he would be deep in counsel
with himself over this matter of ghosts ; and when
late in the evening the van of the Elivi force was
sighted on the east of the village, Bosambo, seated
in state in his magnificent palaver-house, adorned
with such Christmas plates as came his way, awaited
their arrival.

Limberi, the headman, went out to meet the
disgruntled force.

" Chief," he said, " it is our lord's wish that you
leave your spears outside the city."

" Limberi," said Ikifari, a hard man of forty,
all wiry muscle and leanness, " we are people of
your race and your brothers. Why should we
leave our spears—we who are of the Ochori ? "

" You do not come otherwise," said Limberi
decisively. " For across the river are many enemies
of our lord, and he loves you so much, that
for his own protection, he desired your armed
men—your spearmen and your swordsmen—to
sit outside. Thus he will be confident and
happy."

There was no more to be done than to obey.

Ikifari with his counsellors followed the headman
to the palaver, and his insolence was notable.

" I speak for all Elivi," he said, without any
ceremonious preliminaries. " We are an oppressed
people, lord Bosambo, and our young men cry
out with great voices against your cruelty."

" They shall cry louder," said Bosambo, and
Ikifari, the chief, scowled.

" Lord," he said sullenly, " if it is true that

Sandi loves you, he also loves us, and no man is so great in this land that he may stir a people to rebellion."

Bosambo knew this was true—knew it without the muttered approval of Ikifari's headmen. He ran his eye over the little party. They were all there—the malcontents. Tinif'si, the stout headman, M'kera and Calasari, the lesser chiefs; and there was in their minds a certain defiance which particularly exasperated Bosambo. He might punish one or two who set themselves up against his authority, but here was an organised rebellion. Punishment would mean fighting, and fighting would weaken his position with Sanders.

It was the moment to temporise.

Fortunately the devil deputation was not present. It was considered to be against all etiquette for men of another nation to be present at the domestic councils of their neighbours. Otherwise some doubt might have been born in the bosom of Emberi as to the efficacy of Bosambo's devils at this particular moment.

" And this I would say to you, lord," said Ikifari, and Bosambo knew that the crux of the situation would be revealed. " We Elivi are your dogs. You do not send for us to come to your great feasts, nor do you honour us in any way. But when there is fighting you call up our spears and our young men, and you send us abroad to be eaten up by your terrible enemies. Also," he went on, " when you choose your chiefs and counsellors to go pleasant journeys to such places where they are honoured and feasted, you send only men of the Ochori city."

It may be said here that from whatever source Bosambo derived his inspiration, he had certainly acquired royal habits which were foreign to his primitive people. Thus he would dispatch envoys and ambassadors on ceremonious visits bearing gifts and presents which they themselves provided and returning with richer presents which Bosambo acquired. It was, if the truth be told, a novel and pleasant method of extracting blackmail—pleasant because it gave Bosambo little trouble, and afforded his subordinates titillation of importance, and no one had arisen to complain save these unfortunate cities of Akasava—Isisi and N'gombi—which entertained his representatives.

" It is true I have never sent you," said Bosambo, " and my heart is sore at the thought that you should think evil of me because I have saved you all this trouble. For my heart is like water within me. Yet a moon since I sent Kili, my headman, bearing gifts to the king of the bush people, and they chopped him so that he died, and now I fear to send other messengers."

There was an unmistakable sneer on Ikifari's face.

" Lord," he said, with asperity, " Kili was a foolish man and you hated him, for he had spoken evilly against you, stirring up your people. Therefore you sent him to the bushmen and he did not come back." He added significantly : " Now I tell you that if you send me to the bushmen I do not go."

Bosambo thought a moment.

"Now I see," he said, almost jovially, "that Ikifari, whom I love better than my own brother" —this was true—"is angry with me because I have not sent him on a journey. Now I shall show how much I love you, for I will send you all —each of you—as guests of my house, bearing my word to such great nations as the Akasava, the Isisi, the N'gombi; also to the people beyond the river, who are great and give large presents."

He saw the faces brighten, and seized the psychological moment.

"The palaver is finished," said Bosambo magnificently.

He ordered a feast to be made outside the city for his unwelcome guests, and summoned the devil delegates to his presence.

"My friends," he said, "I have given this matter of devils great thought, and since I desire to stand well with you and with your master, I have spent this night in company with six great devils, who are my best friends and who help me in all matters. Now I tell you this—which is known only to myself and to you, whom I trust—that to-day I send to your master six great spirits which inspire me."

There was a hush. The sense of responsibility, which comes to the nervous who are suddenly entrusted with the delivery of a ferocious bull, fell upon the men of the delegation.

"Lord, this is a great honour," said Emberi, "and our masters will send many more presents than your lordship has ever seen. But how may we take these devils with us, for we are fearful and are not used to their ways ? "

Bosambo bowed his head graciously.

" That also filled my thoughts," he said, " and thus I have ordered it. I shall take six of my people—six counsellors and chiefs, who are to me as the sun and the flowers—and by magic I will place inside the heart of each chief and headman one great devil. You shall take these men with you, and you shall listen to all they say save this." He paused. " These devils love me, and they will greatly desire to return to my city and to my land, where they have been so long. Now I tell you that you must treat them kindly. Yet you must hold them, putting a guard about them, and keeping them in a secret place, so that Sandi may not find them and hear of them. And they will bring you fortune and prosperity and the courage of lions."

    •   •   •   •

Sanders was coming up river to settle a woman palaver, when he came slap into a flotilla of such pretension and warlike appearance that he did not hesitate for one moment.

At a word, the canvas jackets were slipped from the Hotchkiss guns, and they were swung over the side. But there was no need for such preparations, as he discovered when Emberi's canoe came alongside.

" Tell me, Emberi," said Sanders, " what is this wonderful thing I see—that the Akasavas and the Isisi, and the N'gombi and the people of the lower forest sail together in love and harmony ? "

" Lord," said Emberi proudly, " this is Bosambo's doing."

Sanders was all suspicion.

" Now I know that Bosambo is a clever man," he said, " yet I did not know that he was so great a character that he could bring together all men in peace, but rather the contrary."

" He has done this because of devils," said Emberi importantly. " Behold, there are certain things about which I must not speak to you, and this is one of them. So, Sandi, ask me no more, for I have sworn an oath."

Leaning over the steamer Sanders surveyed the flotilla. His keen eyes ranged the boat from stem to stern. He noted with interest the presence of one Ikifari, who was known to him. And Ikifari in a scarlet coat was a happy and satisfied man.

" O Ikifari," bantered Sanders, " what of my roads ? "

The chief looked up. " Lord, they shall be made," he said, " though my young men die in the making. I go now to make a grand palaver for my friend and father Bosambo, for he trusts me above all men and has sent me to the Isisi."

Sanders knew something of Bosambo's idiosyncrasies, and nodded.

" When you come back," he said, " I will speak on the matter of these roads. Tell me now, my friend, how long do you stay with the Isisi ? "

" Lord," said Ikifari, " I stay for the time of

a moon. Afterwards I go back to the Ochori,
bearing rich presents which my lord Bosambo
has made me swear I will keep for myself."

" The space of a moon," repeated Sanders.

He turned to ring the engines "Ahead" and
did not see Emberi's hand go up to cover a smile.

CHAPTER XIII

GUNS IN THE AKASAVA

"THANK God!" said the Houssa captain fervently, "there is no war in this country."

"Touch wood!" said Sanders, and the two men simultaneously reached out and laid solemn hands upon the handle of the coffee-pot, which was vulcanite.

If they had touched wood who knows what might have happened in the first place to Ofesi the chief of Mc-Canti?

Who knows what might have happened to the two smugglers of gold from the French territory?

The wife of Bikilini might have gone off with her lover, and Bikilini resigned and patient taken another to wife, and the death men of the Ofesi might never have gone forth upon their unamiable missions, or going forth have been drowned, or grown faint-hearted.

Anyway it is an indisputable fact that neither Sanders nor Captain Hamilton touched wood on the occasion.

And as to Bannister Fish——?

That singular man was a trader in questionable

commodities, for he had not the nice sentiments which usually go with the composition of a white man.

Some say that he ran slaves from Angola to places where a black man or a black woman is worth a certain price; that he did this openly with the connivance of the Government of Portugal and made a tolerable fortune. He certainly bought more poached ivory than any man in Africa, and his crowning infamy up to date was the arming of a South Soudanese Mahdi—arms for employment against his fellow-countrymen.

There are certain manufacturers of small arms in the Midlands who will execute orders to any capacity, produce weapons modern or antiquated at a cost varying with the delicacy or mechanism of the weapon. They have no conscience, but have a hard struggle to pay dividends because there are other firms in Liége who run the same line of business, but produce at from 10 per cent. to 25 per cent. lower cost.

Mr. Bannister Fish, a thin, wiry man of thirty-four, as yellow as a guinea and with the temper of a fiend, was not popular on the coast, especially with officials. Fortunately Africa has many coasts, and since Africa in mass was Mr. Fish's hunting-ground, rather than any particular section, the coast men—as we know the coast—saw little of him.

It was Mr. Fish's boast that there was not twenty miles of coast line from Dakka to Cape-town, and from Lourenço Marques to Suez, that had not contributed something of beauty to his lordly mansion on the top of Highgate Hill.

You will observe that he omits reference to the coast which encloses Cape Colony, and there is a reason. Cape Colony is immensely civilised, has stipendiary magistrates and a horrible breakwater where yellow-jacketed convicts labour for their sins, and Mr. Fish's sins were many. He tackled Sanders's territory in the same spirit as a racehorse breeder will start raising Pekingese poodles—not for the money he could make out of it, but as an amusing sideline.

He worked ruin on the edge of the Akasava country, operating from the adjoining foreign territories, and found an unholy joy in worrying Sanders, whom he had met once and most cordially disliked.

His dislike was intensified on the next occasion of their meeting, for Sanders, making a forced march across the Akasava, seized the caravan of Mr. Bannister Fish, burnt his stores out of hand, and submitted the plutocrat of Highgate Hill to the indignity of marching handcuffed to headquarters. Mr. Fish was tried by a divisional court and fined £500, or, as an alternative, awarded twelve months imprisonment with hard labour.

The fine was paid, and Mr. Fish went home saying horrible things about Mr. Commissioner Sanders, which I will not sully these fair pages by repeating.

Highgate Hill is a prosaic neighbourhood served by prosaic motor-buses, and not the place where one would imagine wholesale murder might be

planned, yet from his domain in Highgate Mr. Fish
issued certain instructions by telephone and cable-
gram, and at his word men went secretly into
Sanders's territory looking for the likely man.

They found Ofesi, and Highgate spoke to the
Akasava to some purpose.

In the month of February in a certain year
Mr. Fish drove resplendently in his electric landau
from Highgate to Waterloo. He arrived on the
Akasava border seven weeks later no less angry
with Sanders than he had ever been, and of a
cheerful countenance because, being a millionaire,
he could indulge in his hobbies, and his hobby
was the annoyance of a far-away Commissioner
who, at that precise moment was touching vulcanite
and thinking it wood.

Ofesi, the son of Malaka, the son of G'nani,
was predestined.

Thus it was predicted by the famous witch-
doctor Komonobologo, of the Akasava.

For it would appear that on the night that Ofesi
came squealing into the world, there were certain
solar manifestations such as an eclipse of the moon
and prodigious shooting of stars, which Komonobologo translated favourably to the clucking, sobbing
and shrill whimpering morsel of whitey-brown
humanity.

Thus Ofesi was to rule all peoples as far as the
sun shone (some three hundred miles in all directions according to local calculations), and he should
not suffer ignominious death at the hand of any
man.

Ofesi (literally " the Born-Lucky ") should be mighty in counsel and in war ; should shake the earth with the tread of his legions ; might risk and gain, never risk and lose ; was the favoured of ju-jus and ghosts ; and would have many sons.

The hollow-eyed woman stretched on the floor of the hut spoke faintly of her happiness, the baby with greedy mouth satisfying the beast in him said nothing, being too much occupied with his natural and instinctive desires.

Such prophecies are common, and some come to nothing. Some, for no apparent reason, stick fast to the recipients.

Ofesi—his destiny—was of the sticking kind.

When Sanders took up his duties on the river, Ofesi was a lank and awkward youth of whom his fellows stood in awe.

Sanders was in awe of nobody. He listened quietly to the recital of portents, omens, and the like, and when it was finished, he delivered a little homily on the fallibility of human things and the extraordinarily high death-rate which existed amongst those misguided people who walked outside the rigid circle of the land.

Ofesi had neighbours more hearty than Sanders, and by these he was accepted as something on account of the total wonder which the years would produce.

So Ofesi grew and flourished, doing much mischief in his way, which was neither innocent nor boyish, and the friendly hand which is upraised to small boys all the world over never fell sharply upon his well-covered nerves, because Ofesi was predestined and immune.

In course of time he was appointed by the then king of the Akasava to the chieftainship of the village of Mi-lanti, and the city of the Akasava breathed a sigh of relief to see his canoe go round the bend of the river out of sight.

No report of the chief's minor misdoings came to Sanders because this legend of destiny carried to all the nations save and except one.

It is said that Ofesi received more homage and held a more regal court in his tiny principality than did the king his master ; that N'gombi, Isisi, and the tribes about sent him presents doubly precious, and that he had a household of sixty wives, all contributed by his devotees. It was also said that he made the intoxicating distributions of Mr. Fish possible, but Sanders had no proof of this.

He raided his friends impartially, did all manner of unpleasant things, terrorised the river from the Lesser Isisi to the edge of the Ochori, and the fishermen watching his war canoes creeping stealthily through the night would say : " Let no man see the lord Ofesi ; lest in the days to come he remember and blind us."

Whether from sheer cunning or from the intuitive faculty which is a part of genius, Ofesi grew to stout manhood without once violating the border line of the Ochori

Until upon a day——

Sanders came in great haste one wet April night

when the clouds hung so low over the river that you might have touched them with a fishing-rod.

It was a night of billowing mists, of drenching cloud bursts, of loud cracking thunders and the flicker-flacker of lightning so incessant that only the darkness counted as interval.

Yet, against the swollen stream, drenched to the skin, his wet face set to the stinging rain and the white rod of his searchlight piercing such gloom as there was, Sanders came as fast as stern wheel could revolve for the Akasava land.

He came up to the village of Mi-lanti in the wild grey of a stormy dawn, and such of the huts as the flooding waters of the heavens had spared stood isolated sentinels amidst smoking ruins.

He landed tired and immensely angry, and found many dead men and one or two who thought they were dead. They told him a doleful story of rapine and murder, of an innocent village set upon by the Ochori and taken in its defencelessness.

"That is a lie," said Sanders promptly, "for you have stockades, built to the west of the village and your dead are all painted as men paint themselves who prepare long for war. Also the Ochori —such as I have seen—are not so painted, which tells me that they came in haste against a warring people."

The wounded man turned his tired face to Sanders.

"It is my faith," he said, in the conventional terminology of his tribe, "that you have eyes like a big cat."

Sanders attended to his injuries and left him and his pitiful fellows in a dry hut. Then he went to look for Bosambo, and found him sitting patiently ten miles up the river. He sat before a steep hill of rock and undergrowth. At the top of the hill was the chief of the village of Mi-lanti, and with him were such of his fighting men as were not at the moment in a happier world.

"Lord, this is true," said Bosambo, "that this dog attacked my river villages and put my men to death and my women to service. So I came down against him, for it is written in the Sura of the Djinn that no man shall live to laugh at his own evil."

"There will be a palaver," said Sanders briefly, and bade the crestfallen chief, Ofesi, to come down and stack his spears. Since it is not in the nature of the native man to speak the truth when his skin is in peril, it goes without saying that both sides lied fearfully, and Sanders, sifting the truth, knew which side lied the least.

"Ofesi," he said, at the end of much weariness of listening, "what do you say that I shall not hang you?"

Ofesi, a short, thick man with a faint beard, looked up and down, left and right for inspiration.

"Lord," he said after a while, "this you know, that all my life I have been a good man—and it is said that I have a high destiny, and shall not die by cruelty."

"'Man is eternal whilst he lives,'" quoted Sanders, "yet man dies sooner or later."

Ofesi stared round at Bosambo, and Bosambo was guilty of an indiscretion—possibly the greatest indiscretion of his life. In the presence of his master, and filled with the exultation and virtuous righteousness which come to the palpably innocent in the face of trial, he said in English, shaking his head the while reprovingly :

" Oh, you dam' naughty devil ! "

Sanders had condemned the man to death in his heart ; had mentally chosen the tree on which the marauding chief should swing when Bosambo spoke.

Sanders had an immense idea as to the sanctity of life in one sense. He had killed many by rope with seeming indifference, and, indeed, he never allowed the question of a man's life or death to influence him one way or the other when an end was in view.

He would watch with unwavering eyes the breath choke out of a swaying body, yet there must be a certain ritual of decency, of fitness, of decorum in such matters, or his delicate sense of justice was outraged.

Bosambo's words, grotesque, uncalled for, wholly absurd, saved the life of Ofesi the chief.

For a moment Sanders's lips twitched irresponsibly, then he turned with a snarl upon the discomfited chief of the Ochori.

" Back to your land, you monkey man ! " he snapped ; " this man has offended against the land—yet he shall live, for he is a fool. I know a greater one ! "

He sent Ofesi back to his village to build up what his folly had overthrown.

" Remember, Ofesi," he said, " I give you back your life, though you deserve death : and I do this because it comes to me suddenly that you are a child as Bosambo is a child. Now, I will come back to you with the early spring, and if you have deserved well of me you shall be rewarded with your liberty ; and if you have done ill to me, you shall go to the Village of Irons or to a worse place."

Back at headquarters Sanders told a sympathetic captain of Houssas the story.

" It was horribly weak of course," he said ; " but, somehow, when that ass Bosambo let rip his infernal English I couldn't hang a sparrow."

" Might have brought this Ofesi person down to the village " said the captain thoughtfully. " He's got an extraordinary reputation."

Sanders sat on the edge of the table, his hands thrust into his breeches pockets.

" I thought of that, too, and it affected me. You see, there was just a fear in my mind that I was being influenced on the wrong side by this fellow's talk of destiny—that I was being, in fact, a little malicious."

The Houssa skipper snapped his cigarette case and looked thoughtful.

" I'll get another company down from headquarters," he said.

" You might ask for a machine-gun section also," said Sanders. " I've got it in my bones that there's going to be trouble.

A week later the upper river saw many strange faces. Isolated fishermen came from nowhere in particular to pursue their mild calling in strange waters.

They built their huts in unfrequented patches of forest, and you might pass up and down a stretch of the beach without knowing that hut was modestly concealed in the thick bush at the back.

Also they went about their business at night with fishing spear and light canoe tacking across river and up river, moving without sound in the shadows of the bank, approaching villages and cities with remarkable circumspection.

They were strange fishermen indeed, for they fished with pigeons. In every canoe the birds drowsed in a wicker-work cage, little red labels about their legs on which even an untutored spy might make a rude but significant mark with the aid of an indelible pencil.

Sanders took no risks.

He summoned Ahmed Ali, the chief of his secret men.

"Go to the Akasava country, and there you will find Ofesi, a chief of the village Mi-lanti. Watch him, for he is an evil man. On the day that he moves against me and my people you shall judge whether I can come in time with my soldiers. If there is time send for me: but if he moves swiftly you shall shoot him dead and you shall not be blamed. Go with God."

"Master," said Ahmed, "Ofesi is already in hell."

If all reports worked out, and they certainly tallied, Ofesi, the predestined chief, gave no offence. He rebuilt his city, chosing higher ground and following a long and unexpected hunting trip, which took him to the edge of the Akasava country, and he projected a visit of love and harmony to Bosambo.

He even sent swift couriers to Sanders to ask permission for the ceremonial, though such permission was wholly unnecessary. Sanders granted the request, delaying the deputation until he had sent his own messengers to Bosambo.

So on a bright June morning Ofesi set forth on his mission, his two and twenty canoes painted red, and even the paddles newly burnt to fantastic and complimentary designs; and he came to the Ochori and was met by Bosambo, a profound sceptic but outwardly pleasant.

"I see you," said Ofesi, "I see you, lord Bosambo, also your brave and beautiful people; yet I come in peace and it grieves me that you should meet me with so many spears."

For in truth the beach bristled a steel welcome and three fighting regiments of the Ochori, gallantly arrayed, were ranked in hollow square, the fourth side of which was the river.

"Lord Ofesi," said Bosambo suavely, "this is the white man's way of doing honour and, as you know, I have much white blood in my veins, being related to the English Prime Minister."

He surveyed the two-and-twenty canoes with their twenty paddlers to each, and duly noted

H

that each paddler carried his fighting spears as a matter of course.

That Ofesi had any sinister design upon the stronghold of the Ochori may be dismissed as unlikely. He was cast in no heroic mould, and abhorred unnecessary risk, for destiny requires some assistance.

He had brought his spears for display rather than for employment. Willy-nilly he must stack them now—an unpleasant operation, reminiscent of another stacking under the cold eye of Sanders.

So it may be said that the *rapprochement* between the Ochori and the Akasava chief began inauspiciously. Bosambo led the way to his guest-house—new-thatched as is the custom.

There was a great feast in Ofesi's honour, and a dance of girls—every village contributing its chief dancer for the event. Next day there was a palaver with sacrifices of fowl and beast, and blood friendships were sworn fluently. Bosambo and Ofesi embraced before all the people assembled, and ate salt from the same dish.

" Now I will tell you all my business, my brother," said Ofesi that night. " To-morrow I go back to my people with your good word, and I shall speak of you by day and night because of your noble heart."

" I also will have no rest," said Bosambo, " till I have journeyed all over this land, speaking about my wonderful brother Ofesi."

With a word Ofesi dismissed his counsellors, and Bosambo, accepting the invitation, sent away his headmen

" Now I will tell you," said Ofesi.

And what he said, what flood of *ego*-oratory, what promises, what covert threats, provided Bosambo with reminiscences for long afterwards.

" Yet," he concluded, " though all things have moved to make me what I am, yet there is much I have to learn, and from none can I learn so well as from you, my brother."

" That is very true," said Bosambo, and meant it.

" Now," Ofesi went on to his peroration, " the king of the Akasava is dying and all men are agreed that I shall be king in his place, therefore I would learn to the utmost grain all the secrets of kingship. Therefore, since I cannot sit with you, I ask you, lord Bosambo, to give a home to Tolinobo, my headman, that he may sit for a year in the shadow of your wisdom and tell me the many beautiful things you say."

Bosambo looked thoughtfully at Tolinobo, the headman, a shifty fisherman promoted to that position, and somewhat deficient in sanity, as Bosambo judged.

" He shall sit with me," said Bosambo at length, " and be as my own son, sleeping in a hut by mine, and I will treat him as if he were my brother."

There was a fleeting gleam of satisfaction in Ofesi's eye as he rose to embrace his blood-friend ; but then he did not know how Bosambo treated his brother.

The Akasava chief and his two and twenty canoes paddled homeward at daybreak, and Bosambo saw them off.

When they were gone, he turned to his headman

"Tell me, Solonkinini," he said, "what have we done with this Tolinobo who stays with us?"

"Lord, we build him a new hut this morning in your lordship's shadow."

Bosambo nodded.

"First," he said, "you shall take him to the secret place near the Crocodile Pool and stake him out. Presently I will come, and we will ask him some questions."

"Lord, he will not answer," said the headman. "I myself have spoken with him."

"He shall answer me," said Bosambo, significantly, "and you shall build a fire and make very hot your spears, for I think this Tolinobo has something he will be glad to tell."

Bosambo's prediction was justified by fact.

Ofesi was not half-way home, happy in his success, when a blubbering Tolinobo, stretched ignominiously on the ground, spoke with a lamentable lack of reserve on all manner of private matters, being urged thereto by a red hot spear-head which Bosambo held much too near his face for comfort.

*   *   *   *

At about this time came Jim Greel, an American adventurer, and Francis E. Coulson, a citizen of the world. They came into Sanders's territory unwillingly, for they were bound, via the French river which skirted the north of the N'gombi land, for German West Africa. There was in normal times a bit of a stream which connected the great river with the Frenchi river. It was, according

to a facetious government surveyor, navigable
for balloons and paper boats except once in a
decade when a mild spring in the one thousand-
miles distant mountains coincided with heavy
rains in the Isisi watershed. Given the coin-
cidence the tiny dribble of rush-choked water
achieved the dignity of riverhood. It was bad
luck that Jim and Coulson hit an exceptional season.

Keeping to the left bank, and moving only
by night—they had reason for this—the adventurers
followed the course of the stream which ordinarily
was not on the map, and they were pardonably
and almost literally at sea.

Two long nights they worked their crazy
little steamer through an unknown territory without realising that it was unknown. They avoided
such villages as they passed, shutting off steam
and dowsing all lights till they drifted beyond
sight and hearing.

At last they reached a stage in their enterprise
where the maintenance of secrecy was a matter
of some personal danger, and they looked around
in the black night for assistance.

"Looks like a village over there, Jim," said
Coulson, and the steersman nodded.

"There's shoal water here," he said grimly,
"and the forehold is up to water-level."

"Leakin'?"

"Not exactly leakin'," said Jim carefully; "but
there's no bottom to the forepart of this tub."

Coulson swore softly at the African night. The
velvet darkness had fallen on them suddenly, and

It was a case of tie-up or go on—Jim decided to go on.

They had struck a submerged log and ripped away the bottom of the tiny compartment that was magniloquently called " No. 1 hold "; the bulkhead of Nos. 1 and 2 was of the thinnest steel and was bulging perceptibly.

Coulson did not know this, but Jim did.

Now he turned the prow of the ancient steamer to the dark shore, and the revolving paddle-wheels made an expiring effort.

Somewhere on the river bank a voice called to them in the Akasava tongue; they saw the fires of the village, and black shadows passing before them; they heard women laughing.

Jim turned his head and gave an order to one of his naked crew, and the man leapt overboard with a thin rope hawser.

Then the ripped keel of the little boat took the sand and she grounded.

Jim lit his pipe from a lantern that hung in the deck cabin behind him, wiped his streaming forehead with the back of his hand, and spoke rapidly in the Akasava tongue to the little crowd who had gathered on the beach. He spoke mechanically, warning all and sundry for the safety of their immortal souls not to slip his hawser : warning them that if he lost so much as a deck rivet he would flay alive the thief, and ended by commending his admiring audience to M'shimba M'shamba, Bim-bi, O'kill, and such local devils as he could call to his tongue.

" That's let me out," he said, and waded ashore
through the shallow water as one too much overcome by the big tragedies of life to care very
much one way or another whether he was wet or
dry.

He strode up the shelving beach and was led
by a straggling group of villagers to the headman's
hut to make inquiries, and came back to the boat
with unpleasant news.

Coulson had brought her nose to the sand, and
by a brushwood fire that the men of the village
had lit upon the beach, the damage was plainly
to be seen.

The tiny hull had torn like brown paper, and part
of the cause—a stiff branch of gun-wood—still
protruded from the hole.

" We're in Sanders's territory, if it's all the same
to you," said Jim gloomily. " The damnation
old Frenchi river is in spruit and we've come
about eighty miles on the wrong track."

Coulson, kneeling by the side of the boat, a
short, black briar clutched between his even white
teeth, looked up with a grin.

"' Sande catchee makee hell,'" quoted he. " Do
you remember the Chink shaver who used to run
the Angola women up to the old king for Bannister
Fish ? "

Jim said nothing. He took a roll of twist from
his pocket, bit off a section, and chewed philosophically.

" There's no slavery outfit in *this* packet," he
said. " I guess even old man Fish wouldn't fool

'round in this land—may the devil grind him for bone-meal ! "

There was no love lost between the amiable adventurers and Mr. Bannister Fish. That gentleman himself, sitting in close conference with Ofesi not fifty miles from whence the *Grasshopper* lay, would have been extremely glad to know that her owners were where they were.

" Fish is out in these territories for good," said Jim ; " but it'll do us no good—our not bein' Fish, I mean, if Sandi comes nosing round lookin' for traders' licences—somehow I don't want anybody to inspect our cargo."

Coulson nodded as he wielded a heavy hammer on the damaged plate.

" I guess he'll know all right," Jim went on. " You can't keep these old *lokalis* quiet—listen to the joyous news bein', so to speak, flashed forth to the expectant world."

Coulson suspended his operations. Clear and shrill came the rattle of the *lokali* tapping its message :

" Tom-te tom, tom-te tom, tommitty tommitty tommitty-tom."

" There she goes," said the loquacious Jim, complacently. " Two white men of suspicious appearance have arrived in town—Court papers please copy."

Coulson grinned again. He was working his hammer deftly, and already the offending branch had disappeared.

"A ha'porth of cement in the morning," he said, "and she's the Royal yacht."

Jim sniffed.

"It'll take many ha'porths of cement to make her anything but a big intake pipe," he said. He put his hand on the edge of the boat and leapt aboard. Abaft the deck-house were two tiny cupboards of cabins, the length of a man's body and twice his width. Into one of these he dived, and returned shortly afterwards with a small, worn portmanteau, patched and soiled. He jumped down over the bows to the beach, first handing the piece of baggage down to the engineer of the little boat. It was so heavy that the man nearly dropped it.

"What's the idea ? " Coulson mopped the sweat from his forehead with a pocket-handkerchief, and turned his astonished gaze to the other.

" 'Tis the loot," said Jim significantly. "We make a cache of this to-night lest a worse thing happen.

"Oh, God, this man ! " prayed Coulson, appealing heavenward. " With the eyes of the whole dam' barbarian rabble directed on him, he stalks through the wilderness with his grip full of gold and his heart full of innocent guile ! "

Jim refilled his pipe leisurely from a big, leather pouch that hung at his waist before he replied. " Coulson," he said between puffs, " in the language of that ridiculous vaudeville artiste we saw before we quit London, you may have brains in your head, but you've got rabbit's blood in your feet.

There's no occasion for getting scared, only I surmise that one of your fellow-countrymen will be prowling around here long before the bows of out stately craft take the water like a thing of life, and since he is the Lord High Everything in this part of the world, and can turn out a man's pocket without so much as a ' damn ye,' I am for removing all trace of the Frenchi Creed River diggings."

Coulson had paused in his work, and sat squatting on his heels, his eyes fixed steadily on his partner's. He was a good-looking young man of twenty-seven, a few years the junior of the other, whose tanned face was long and thin, but by no means unpleasant.

" What does it matter ? " asked Coulson after a while. " He can only ask where we got the dust, and we needn't tell him ; and if we do we've got enough here to keep us in comfort all our days."

Jim smiled.

" Suppose he holds this gold ? " he asked quietly. " Suppose he just sends his spies along to discover where the river digging is—and suppose he finds it is in French territory and that there is a prohibitive export duty from the French country. Oh ! there's a hundred suppositions, and they're all unpleasant."

Coulson rose stiffly.

" I think we'll take the risk of the boat foundering, Jim," he said. " Put the grip back."

Jim hesitated, then with a nod he swung the portmanteau aboard and followed. A few minutes later he was doubled up in the perfectly inadequate space of No. 1 hold, swabbing out the ooze of the river, and singing in a high falsetto the love song of a mythical Bedouin.

It was past midnight when the two men, tired, aching, and cheerful, sought their beds.

" If Sanders turns up," shouted Jim as he arranged his mosquito curtain (the shouting was necessary, since he was addressing his companion through a matchboard partition between the two cabins), " you've got to lie, Coulson."

" I hate lying," grumbled Coulson loudly; " but I suppose we shall have to ? "

" Betcher ! " yawned the other, and said his prayers with lightning rapidity.

Daylight brought dismay to the two voyagers.

The hole in the hull was not alone responsible for the flooded hold. There was a great gash in her keel—the plate had been ripped away by some snag or snags unknown. Coulson looked at Jim, and Jim returned the despairing gaze.

" A canoe for mine," said Jim after a while. " Me for the German river and so home. That is the way I intended moving, and that is the way I go."

Coulson shook his head.

" Flight ! " he said briefly. " You can explain being in Sanders's territory, but you can't explain the bolt—stick it out ! "

All that morning the two men laboured in the hot sun to repair the damage. Fortunately the cement was enough to stop up the bottom leak, and there was enough over to make a paste with

twigs and sun-dried sand to stop the other. But
there was no blinking the fact that the protection
afforded was of the frailest. The veriest twig
embedded in a sandbank would be sufficient to
pierce the flimsy " plating." This much the two
men saw when the repairs were completed at the
end of the day. The hole in the bow could only
be effectively dealt with by the removal of one
plate and the substitution of another, " and that,"
said Jim, " can hardly happen."

The German river was eighty miles upstream
and a flooded stream that ran five knots an hour
at that. Allow a normal speed of nine knots to
the tiny *Grasshopper*, and you have a twenty hours'
run at best.

" The river's full of floatin' timber," said Jim
wrathfully, eyeing the swift sweep of the black
waters, " an' we stand no better chance of gettin'
anywhere except to the bottom ; it's a new plate
or nothing."

Thus matters stood with a battered *Grasshopper*
high and dry on the shelving beach of the Akasava
village, and two intrepid but unhappy gold smugglers
discussing ways and means, when complications
occurred which did much to make the life of Mr.
Commissioner Sanders unbearable.

*   *   *   *

There was a woman of the Akasava who bore
the name of Ufambi, which means a " bad woman."
She had a lover—indeed, she had many, but the
principal was a hunter named Logi. He was a
tall, taciturn man, and his teeth were sharpened

to two points. He was broad-shouldered, his hair was plastered with clay, and he wore a cloak that was made from the tails of monkeys. For this reason he was named Logi N'kemi, that is to say, Logi the Monkey.

He had a hut far in the woods, three days' journey, and in this wood were several devils; therefore he had few visitors.

Ufambi loved this man exceedingly, and as fervently hated her husband, who was a creature of Ofesi. Also, he was not superior to the use of the stick.

One day Ufambi annoyed him and he beat her. She flew at him like a wild cat and bit him, but he shook her off and beat her the more, till she ran from the hut to the cool and solitary woods, for she was not afraid of devils.

Here her lover found her, sitting patiently by the side of the forest path, her well-moulded arms hugging her knees, her chin sunk, a watchful, brooding and an injured woman.

They sat together and talked, and the woman told him all there was to be told, and Logi the Monkey listened in silence.

" Furthermore," she went on, " he has buried beneath the floor of the hut certain treasures given to him by white men, which you may take."

She said this pleadingly, for he had shown no enthusiasm in the support of her plan.

" Yet how can I kill your husband," said Logi, carefully, " and if I do kill him and Sandi comes here, how may I escape his cruel vengeance? I think it would be better if you gave him death in his chop, for then none would think evilly of me.'

She was not distressed at his patent selfishness. It was understandable that a man should seek safety for himself, but she had no intention of carrying out her lover's plan.

She returned to her husband, and found him so far amiable that she escaped a further beating. Moreover, he was communicative.

"Woman," he said, "to-morrow I go a long journey because of certain things I have seen, and you go with me. In a secret place, as you know, I have hidden my new canoe, and when it is dark you shall take as much fish and my two little dogs and sit in the canoe waiting for me."

"I will do this thing, lord," she said meekly.

He looked at her for a long time.

"Also," he said after a while, "you shall tell no man that I am leaving, for I do not desire that Sandi shall know, though," he added, "if all things be true that Ofesi says, he will know nothing."

"I will do this as you tell me, lord," said the woman.

He rose from the floor of the hut where he had been squatting and went out of the hut.

"Come!" he said graciously, and she followed him to the beach and joined the crowd of villagers who watched two white men labouring under difficulties.

By and by she saw her husband detach himself

from the group and make his cautious way to where the white men were.

Now Bikilari—such was the husband's name—was a N'gombi man, and the N'gombi folk are one of two things, and more often than not, both. They are either workers in iron or thieves, and Jim, looking up at the man, felt a little spasm of satisfaction at the sight of the lateral face marks which betrayed his nationality.

" Ho, man ! " said Jim in the vernacular, " what are you that you stand in my sun ? "

" I am a poor man, lord," said Bikilari, " and I am the slave of all white men : now I can do things which ignorant men cannot, for I can take iron and bend it by heat, also I can bend it without heat, as my fathers and my tribe have done since the world began."

Coulson watched the man keenly, for he was no lover of the N'gombi.

" Try him out, Jim," he said, so they gave Bikilari a hammer and some strips of steel, and all the day he worked strengthening the rotten bow of the *Grasshopper*.

In the evening, tired and hungry, he went back to his hut for food ; but his wife had watched him too faithfully for his comfort, and the cooking-pot was cold and empty. Bikilari beat her with his stick, and for two hours she sobbed and blew upon the embers of the fire alternately whilst my lord's fish stewed and spluttered over her bent head

       *   *   *   *

Jim was a good sleeper but a light one. He woke on the very smell of danger. Here was something more tangible than scent—a dog-like scratching at his door. In the faint moonlight he saw a figure crouching in the narrow alley-way, saw, too, by certain conformations, that it was a woman, and drew an uncharitable conclusion. Yet, since she desired secrecy, he was willing to observe her wishes. He slid back the gauze door and flickered an electric lamp (most precious possession, to be used with all reserve and economy). She shrank back at this evidence of magic and breathed an entreaty.

" What do you want ? " he asked in a low voice.

" Lord," she answered, her voice muffled, " if you desire your life, do not stay here."

Jim thrust his face nearer to the woman's.

" Say what you must say very quickly," he said.

" Lord," she began again, " my husband is Bikilari, a worker in iron. He is the man of Ofesi, and to-night Ofesi sends his killers to do his work upon all white men and upon all chiefs who thwart him. Also upon you because you are white and there is treasure in your ship."

" Wait," said Jim, and turned to tap on Coulson's door. There was no need. Coulson was out of bed at the first sound of whispering and now stood in the doorway, the moonlight reflected in a cold blue line on the revolver he held in his hand.

" It may be a fake—but there's no reason why

It should be," he said when the story was told. " We'll chance the hole in the bow."

Jim ran forward and woke the sleeping engineer, and came back with the first crackle of burning wood in the furnace.

He found the woman waiting.

" What is your name ? " he asked.

She stood with her back to the tiny rail, an easy mark for the man who had followed her and now crouched in the shadow of the hull. He could reach up and touch her. He slipped out his long N'gombi hunting knife and felt the point.

" Lord," said the woman, " I am——"

Then she slipped down to the deck.

Coulson fired twice at the fleeing Bikilari, and missed him. Logi, the lover, leapt at him from the beach but fell before a quick knife-thrust.

Bikilari reached the bushes in safety and plunged into the gloom—and into the arms of Ahmed Ali, a swift, silent man, who caught the knife arm in one hand and broke the neck of the murderer with the other—for Ahmed Ali was a famous wrestler in the Kono country.

The city was aroused, naked feet pattered through the street. Jim and Coulson, lying flat on the bow of the steamer, held the curious at bay.

Two hours they lay thus whilst the cold boilers generated energy. Then the paddle wheel threshed desperately astern, and the *Grasshopper* dragged herself to deep water.

A figure hailed them from the bank in Swaheli.

" Lord," it said, " go you south and meet Sandi

—northward is death, for the Isisi are up and the Akasava villagers are in their canoes—also all white men in this land are dead, save Sandi."

"Who are you?" megaphoned Jim, and the answer came faintly as the boat drifted to midstream.

"I am Ahmed Ali, the servant of Sandi, whom may God preserve!"

"Come with us!" shouted Jim.

The figure on the bank, clear to be seen in his white jellab, made a trumpet of his hands.

"I go to kill one Ofesi, according to orders—say this to Sandi."

Then the boat drifted beyond earshot.

"Up stream or down?" demanded Jim at the wheel. "Down we meet Sanders and up we meet the heathen in his wrath."

"Up," said Coulson, and went aft to count noses.

That night died Iliki, the chief of the Isisi, and I'mini, his brother, stabbed as they sat at meat, also Bosomo of the Little Isisi, and B'ramo of the N'gomi, chiefs all; also the wives and sons of B'ramo and Bosomo; Father O'Leary of the Jesuit Mission at Mosankuli, his lay minister, and the Rev. George Calley, of the Wesleyan Mission at Bogori, and the Rev. Septimus Keen and his wife, at the Baptist Mission at Michi.

Bosambo did not die, because he knew; also a certain headman of Ofesi knew—and died.

Ofesi had planned largely and well. War had come to the territories in the most terrible form, yet Bosambo did not hesitate, though he was aware of his inferiority, not only in point of numbers, but in the more important matter of armament.

For the most dreadful thing had happened, and pigeons flying southward from a dozen points carried the news to Sanders—for the first time in history the rebellious people of the Akasava were armed with rifles—rifles smuggled across the border and placed in the hands of Ofesi's warriors.

The war-drum of the Ochori sounded. At dawn Bosambo led forty war canoes down the river, seized the first village that offered resistance and burnt it. He was for Ofesi's stronghold, and was half-way there when he met the tiny *Grasshopper* coming up stream.

At first he mistook it for the *Zaire* and made little effort to disclose the pacific intentions of his forty canoes, but a whistling rifle bullet aimed precisely made him realise the danger of taking things for granted.

He paddled forward alone, ostentatiously peaceable, and Jim received him.

" Rifles ? "   Coulson was incredulous.   " O chief, you are mad ! "

" Lord," said Bosambo earnestly, " let Sandi say if I be mad—for Sandi is my bro—is my master and friend," he corrected himself.

Jim knew of Bosambo—the chief enjoyed a reputation along the coast, and trusted him now.

He turned to his companion.

" If all Bosambo says is true there'll be hell in this country," he said quietly. " We can't cut and run. Can you use a rifle ? " he asked.

Bosambo drew himself up.

" Suh," he said in plain English, " I make 'um shoot plenty at Cape Coast Cassell—I shoot 'um two bulls' eyes out."

Coulson considered.

" We'll cashee that gold," he said. " It would be absurd to take that with us. O Bosambo, we have a great treasure, and this we will leave in your city."

" Lord," said Bosambo quietly, " it shall be as my own treasure."

" That's exactly what I don't want it to be," said Coulson.

The fleet waited whilst Bosambo returned to Ochori city with the smugglers ; there, in Bosambo's hut, and in a cunningly-devised hole beneath the floor, the portmanteau was hidden and the *Grasshopper* went joyfully with the stream to whatever adventures awaited her.   :

*   *   *   *

The moonlight lay in streaks of sage and emerald green—such a green as only the moon, beheld through the mists of the river, can show. Sage green for shadow, bright emerald on the young spring verdure, looking from light to dark or from dark to light, as the lazy breezes stirred the undergrowth. In the gleam of the moonlight there was one bright, glowing speck of red—it was the end of Mr. Commissioner Sanders's cigar.

He sat in the ink-black shadow cast by the awning on the foredeck of the *Zaire*. His feet, encased in long, pliant mosquito boots that reached to his knees, rested on the rail of the boat, and he was a picture of contentment and cheerful idleness.

An idle man might be restless. You might expect to hear the creak of the wicker chair as he changed his position ever so slightly, yet it is a strange fact that no such sound broke the pleasant stillness of the night.

He sat in silence, motionless. Only the red tip of the cigar glowed to fiery brightness and dulled to an ashen red as he drew noiselessly at his cheroot.

A soft felt hat, pulled down over his eyes, would have concealed the direction of his gaze, even had the awning been removed. His lightly clasped hands rested over one knee, and but for the steady glow of the cigar he might have been asleep.

Yet Sanders of the River was monstrously awake. His eyes were watching the tousled bushes by the water's edge, roving from point to point, searching every possible egress.

There was somebody concealed in those bushes— as to that Sanders had no doubt. But why did they wait—for it was a case of " they "— and why, if they were hostile, had they not attacked him before ?

Sanders had had his warnings. Some of the pigeons came before he had left headquarters ; awkwardly scrawled red labels had set the bugles ringing through the Houssa quarters. But he had missed the worst of the messages. Bosambo's all-Arabic exclamation had fallen into the talons of a watchful hawk—poor winged messenger and all.

Sanders rose swiftly and silently. Behind him

was the open door of his cabin, and he stepped in, walked in the darkness to the telephone above the head of his bunk and pressed a button.

Abiboo dozing with his head against the buzzer answered instantly.

" Let all men be awakened," said Sanders in a whisper. " Six rifles to cover the bush between the two dead trees."

" On my head," whispered Abiboo, and settled his tarboosh more firmly upon that section of his anatomy,

Sanders stood by the door of his cabin, a sporting Lee-Enfield in the crook of his arm, waiting.

Then from far away he heard a faint cry, a melancholy, shrill whoo-wooing. It was the cry that set the men of the villages shuddering, for it was such a cry as ghosts make.

Men in the secret service of Sanders, and the Government also, made it, and Sanders nodded his head.

Here came a man in haste to tell him things.

A long pause and " Whoo-woo ! " drearily, plaintively, and nearer. The man was whooing then at a jog-trot, and they on the bank were waiting——

" Fire ! " cried Sanders sharply.

Six rifles crashed like a thunderclap, there was a staccato flick-flack as the bullets struck the leaves, and two screams of anguish.

Out of the bush blundered a dark figure, looked about dazed and uncertain, saw the *Zaire* and raised his hand.

Bang !

A bullet smacked viciously past Sanders's head.

" Guns ! " said Sanders with a gasp, and as the man on the bank rattled back the lever of his repeater, Sanders shot him.

" Bang ! bang ! "

This time from the bush, and the Houssas answered it. Forty men fired independently at the patch of green from whence the flashes had come.

Forty men and more leapt into the water and waded ashore, Sanders at their head.

The ambush had failed. Sanders found three dead men of the Isisi and one slightly injured and quite prepared for surrender.

" Männlichers ! " said Sanders, examining the rifles, and he whistled.

" Lord," said the living of the four, " we did what we were told ; for it is an order that no man shall come to you with tidings ; also, on a certain night that we should shoot you."

" Whose order ? " demanded Sanders.

" Our lord Ofesi's," said the man. " Also, it is an order from a certain white lord who dwells with his people on the border of the land."

They were speaking when the whoo-ing messenger came up at a jog-trot, too weary to be cautioned by the sound of guns.

He was a tired man, dusty, almost naked, and he carried a spear and a cleft-stick.

Sanders read the letter which was stuck therein. It was in ornamental Arabic, and was from Ahmed Ali.

He read it carefully ; then he spoke.

" What do you know of this ? " he asked.

" Lord," said the tired man, flat on the bare ground and breathing heavily, " there is war in this land such as we have never seen, for Ofesi has guns and has slain all chiefs by his cunning ; also there is a white man whom he visits secretly in the forest."

Sanders turned back to the *Zaire*, sick at heart. All these years he had kept his territories free from an expeditionary force, building slowly towards the civilisation which was every administrator's ideal. This meant a punitive force, the introduction of a new régime. The coming of armed white men against these children of his.

Who supplied the arms ? He could not think. He had never dreamt of their importation. His people were too poor, had too little to give.

" Lord," called the resting messenger, as Sanders turned, " there are two white men in a puc-a-puc who rest by the Akasava city."

Sanders shook his head.

These men—who knew them by name ?—were smugglers of gold, who had come through a swollen river by accident. (His spies were very efficient, be it noted.)

Whoever it was, the mischief was done.

" Steam," he said briefly to the waiting Abiboo.

" And this man, lord ? " asked the Houssa, pointing to the last of the would-be assassins.

Sanders walked to the man.

" Tell me," he said, " how many were you who waited to kill me ? "

" Five, lord," said the man.

" Five ? " said Sanders, " but I found only four bodies."

It was at that instant that the fifth man fired from the bank.

*   *   *   *

The *Grasshopper*, towing forty war canoes of the Ochori, came round a bend of the great river and fell into an ambuscade.

The Ochori were a brave people, but unused to the demoralising effect of firearms, however badly and wildly aimed.

Bosambo from the stern of the little steamer yelled directions to his panic-stricken fleet without effect. They turned and fled, paddling for their lives the way they had come. Jim essayed a turning movement in the literal sense, and struck a submerged log   The ill-fated *Grasshopper* went down steadily by the bow, and in a last desperate effort ran for the shore under a hail of bullets.   They leapt to land, four men—Bosambo's fighting headman was the fourth—and, shooting down immediate opposition, made for the bush.

But they were in the heart of the enemy's land —within shooting distance of the Akasava city. Long before they had crossed the league of wood, the *lokali* had brought reinforcements to oppose them. They were borne down by sheer weight of numbers at a place called Iffsimori, and that night came into the presence of the great King Ofesi, the Predestined.

They came, four wounded and battered men

bound tightly with cords of grass, spared for the great king's sport.

" O brother," greeted Ofesi in the face of all his people, " look at me and tell me what has become of Tobolono, my dear headman ? "

Bosambo, his face streaked with dried blood, stared at him insolently.

" He is in hell," he said, " being *majiki* " (predestined).

" Also you will be in hell," said the king, " because men say that you are Sandi's brother."

Bosambo was taken aback for a moment.

" It is true," he said, " that I am Sandi's brother ; for it seems that this is not the time for a man to deny him. Yet I am Sandi's brother only because all men are brothers, according to certain white magic I learnt as a boy."

Ofesi sat before the door of his hut, and it was noticeable that no man stood or sat nearer to him than twenty paces distant.

Jim, glancing round the mob, which surrounded the palaver, saw that every other man carried a rifle, and had hitched across his naked shoulders a canvas cartridge-belt. He noticed, too, now and then, the king would turn his head and speak, as it were, to the dark interior of the hut.

Ofesi directed his gaze to the white prisoners.

" O white men," he said, " you see me now, a great lord, greater than any white man has ever been, for all the little chiefs of this land are dead, and all people say ' Wah, king,' to Ofesi."

" I dare say," said Coulson in English.

" To-night," the king went on, " we sacrifice you, for you are the last white men in this land—Sandi being dead."

" Ofesi, you lie ! "

It was Bosambo, his face puckered with rage, his voice shrill.

" No man can kill Sandi," he cried, " for Sandi alone of all men is beyond death, and he will come to you bringing terror and worse than death ! "

Ofesi made a gesture of contempt.

He waved his hand to the right and as at a signal the crowd moved back.

Bosambo held himself tense, expecting to see the lifeless form of his master. But it was something less harrowing he saw—a prosaic stack of wooden boxes six feet high and eight feet square.

" Ammunition," said Jim under his breath. " The devil had made pretty good preparation."

" Behold ! " said Ofesi, " therein is Sanders' death—listen all people ! "

He held up his hand for silence.

Bosambo heard it—that faint rattle of the *lokali*. From some far distant place it was carrying the news. " Sanders dead ! " it rolled mournfully, " distantly—moonlight—puc-a-puc—middle of river —man on bank—boat at shore—Sandi dead on ground—many wounds." He pieced together the tidings. Sandi had been shot from the bank and the boat had landed him dead. The chief of the Ochori heard the news and wept.

" Now you shall smell death," said Ofesi.

He turned abruptly to the door of the hut and

exchanged a dozen quick words with the man inside. He spoke imperiously, sharply.

Alas! Mr. Bannister Fish, guest of honour on the remarkable occasion, the Ofesi you deal with now is not the meek Ofesi with whom you drove your one-sided bargain in the deep of the Akasava forest! Camel-train and boat have brought ammunition and rifles piecemeal to your enemy's undoing. Ofesi owes his power to you, but the maker of tyrants was ever a builder if his own prison-house.

Mr. Fish felt his danger keenly, pulled two long-barrelled automatic pistols from his pocket and mentally chose his route for the border, cursing his own stupidity that he had not brought his Arab bodyguard along the final stages of the journey.

"Ofesi," he muttered, "there shall be no killing until I am gone."

"Fisi," replied the other louder, "you shall see all that I wish you to see," and he made a signal.

They stripped the white men as naked as they were on the day they were born, pegged them at equal distance on the ground spread-eagle fashion. Heads to the white man's feet they laid Bosambo and his headman.

When all was finished Ofesi walked over to them.

"When the sun comes up," he said, "you will all be dead—but there is half the night to go."

"Nigger!" said Bosambo in English, "yo' mother done be washerwomans!"

It was the most insulting expression in his vocabulary, and he reserved it for the last.

*   *   *   *

Sanders saw the glow of the great fire long before he reached the Akasava, his own *lokali* sounding forth the news of his premature decease—Sanders with the red weal of a bullet across his cheek, and a feeling of unfriendliness toward Ofesi in his heart. All the way up the river through the night his *lokali* sent forth the joyless tidings. Villagers heard it and shivered—but sent it on. A half-naked man crouching in the bushes near Akasava city heard it and sobbed himself sick, for Ahmed Ali saw in himself a murderer. He who had sworn by the prophet to end the life of Ofesi had left the matter until it was too late.

In a cold rage he crept nearer to the crowd which was gathered about the king's hut—a neck-craning, tip-toeing crowd of vicious men-children. The moment of torment had come. At Ofesi's feet crouched two half-witted Akasava youths giggling at one another in pleasurable excitement, and whetting the razor-keen edges of their skinning knives on their palms.

" Listen, now," said Ofesi in exultation. " I am he, the predestined, the ruler of all men from the black waters to the white mountains. Thus you see me, all people, your master, and master of white men. The skins of these men shall be drums to call all other nations to the service of the Akasava —begin Ginin and M'quasa."

The youths rose and eyed the silent victims critically—and Mr. Bannister Fish stepped out of the hut into the light of the fire, a pistol in each hand.

"Chief," said he, " this matter ends here. Release those men or you die very soon."

Ofesi laughed.

"Too late, lord Fisi," he said, and nodded his head.

One shot rang out from the crowd—a man, skilled in the use of arms, had waited for the gun-runner's appearance. Bannister Fish, of Highgate Hill, pitched forward dead.

" Now," said Ofesi.

Ahmed Ali came through the crowd like a cyclone, but quicker far was the two-pound shell of a Hotchkiss gun. Looking upward into the moonlit vault of the sky, Jim saw a momentary flash of light, heard the " pang ! " of the gun and the whine of the shell as it curved downward ; heard a roar louder than any, and was struck senseless by the sharp edge of an exploded cartridge-box.

    *   *   *   *

" Ofesi," said Sanders, " I think this is your end."

" Lord, I think so too," said Ofesi.

Sanders let him hang for two hours before he cut him down.

" Mr. Sanders," said Jim, dressed in a suit of the Commissioner's clothes which fitted none too well, " we ought to explain——"

" I understand," said Sanders with a smile. " Gold smuggling ! "

Jim nodded.

" And where is your gold—at the bottom of the river ? "

It was in the American's heart to lie, but he shook

his head. "The chief Bosambo is holding it for me," he confessed.

"H'm!" said Sanders. "Do you know to an ounce how much you have?"

Coulson shook his head.

"Where is Bosambo?" asked Sanders of his orderly.

"Lord, he has gone in haste to his city with twenty paddlers," said Abiboo.

Sanders looked at Jim queerly.

"You had better go in haste, too," he said dryly. "Bosambo has views of his own on portable property."

"We wept for you," said the indignant Jim, something of a sentimentalist.

"You'll be weeping for yourself if you don't hurry," said the practical Sanders.

THE END.

Lightning Source UK Ltd.
Milton Keynes UK
171125UK00001B/3/A